The Executioner rolled out of the shadows, Beretta up and chugging

Bolan made quick work of putting them in their resting place. He closed the lid on the coffin and leathered the Beretta. Retreating, he checked the parking lot. Before coming in, the soldier had considered fixing the fleet of fancy wheels with plastic explosives, but just as quickly dismissed the idea. This was a commercial and residential neighborhood and no one on the block needed to pay indirectly for the crimes of these savages by finding their homes and businesses pummeled and damaged by raining debris.

Melting into the deeper shadows of the alley, Bolan determined that for all enemies concerned, reality was only just beginning to heat up.

MACK BOLAN ®
The Executioner

The Executioner®
Don Pendleton's

POISON
JUSTICE

A GOLD EAGLE BOOK FROM
W**O**RLDWIDE®

TORONTO • NEW YORK • LONDON
AMSTERDAM • PARIS • SYDNEY • HAMBURG
STOCKHOLM • ATHENS • TOKYO • MILAN
MADRID • WARSAW • BUDAPEST • AUCKLAND

First edition March 2005
ISBN 0-373-64316-0

Special thanks and acknowledgment to
Dan Schmidt for his contribution to this work.

POISON JUSTICE

Even in theory the gas mask is a dreadful thing.
It stands for one's first flash of insight into
man's measureless malignity against man.
—Reginald Farrer 1880–1920
The Void of War

I have seen the terrible result of greed and betrayal.
I have seen the innocent poisoned by evil. It is my
duty to provide those victims with justice.
—Mack Bolan

THE
MACK BOLAN®
LEGEND

Nothing less than a war could have fashioned the destiny of the man called Mack Bolan. Bolan earned the Executioner title in the jungle hell of Vietnam.

But this soldier also wore another name—Sergeant Mercy. He was so tagged because of the compassion he showed to wounded comrades-in-arms and Vietnamese civilians.

Mack Bolan's second tour of duty ended prematurely when he was given emergency leave to return home and bury his family, victims of the Mob. Then he declared a one-man war against the Mafia.

He confronted the Families head-on from coast to coast, and soon a hope of victory began to appear. But Bolan had broken society's every rule. That same society started gunning for this elusive warrior—to no avail.

So Bolan was offered amnesty to work within the system against terrorism. This time, as an employee of Uncle Sam, Bolan became Colonel John Phoenix. With a command center at Stony Man Farm in Virginia, he and his new allies—Able Team and Phoenix Force—waged relentless war on a new adversary: the KGB.

But when his one true love, April Rose, died at the hands of the Soviet terror machine, Bolan severed all ties with Establishment authority.

Now, after a lengthy lone-wolf struggle and much soul-searching, the Executioner has agreed to enter an "arm's-length" alliance with his government once more, reserving the right to pursue personal missions in his Everlasting War.

Prologue

The future belonged to the sociopath.

Spoken by his predecessor—before the black magic baton for head of Special Action Division was passed on to him—Richard Grogen recalled the statement for reasons that pertained to more than his own world. Cradling his HK MP-5 subgun with laser sight and sound suppressor, he believed there was no hidden meaning in the cryptic statement, no warning prophecy. Aware his hold on power was tenuous, at best, he knew both professional and personal fate hedged on the whims and paranoid myopia of faceless powerful shadow men, any of whom called the shots from about three thousand miles east. And, like him, they had more to lose than just careers, if the truth about their black project leaked out for public devouring or congressional cannibalizing. No crystal ball gazing was needed for Grogen to know phantoms would arise in the middle of some future midnight. They would come, shipped out of nowhere to make sure he, too, took all his secrets with him to an unmarked desert grave.

Given what he knew about Project Light Year, aware of the nature of the beast he was chained to, Grogen supposed they believed his fate was inevitable. But, where there was a will to fight, nothing was ever carved in stone. If he was going to retire, it would be on his terms.

Starting now.

He peered ahead into the darkness, absorbing the jounce and pitch of the Hummer from the shotgun seat as it rolled along at a scorpion's pace, wheels catching ruts and furrows, here and there, in the dirt track. The future was somewhere ahead in the utter blackness, but he'd be damned if he could find any sign of life, beyond the combined fanning glow of headlights from the trailing vehicles. The travel brochures claimed Nevada trooped in some thirty million visitors a year, ranking it ahead of Orlando, Florida, as the country's number-one tourist mecca. Naturally, Vegas, Reno and Tahoe gobbled up the lion's share of human life. But out here, Grogen thought, pushing for the Arizona border, where giant prehistoric reptiles, mastodons and woolly mammoths once trod, he might as well be on another planet.

This turf was rumored to have seen more visitors of extraterrestrial origin than human. A younger Grogen, he thought, the Green Beret with a wife and kids to consider—all of whom had abandoned his ship in recent years—would have scoffed it off as so much fantastic rubbish fabricated by local desert rats and freelancing journalists broke, hungry and eager for a sensational story.

He'd heard the wild tales from Area 51—recently emptied of men and material. But, relocated to his new classified base of operations, these days he could be sure they were building—and hiding—more than just the prototype fighter jet for the next generation. And after bearing recent eyewitness to an event he could not comprehend in earthly terms, he began to believe the truth was, indeed, stranger than any fiction.

Grogen felt his driver, Conklin, tensing up, then saw the ex-Delta commando throw him a look. The hero's lips were parting to fire off questions. He could almost read the man's thoughts, the mind rife with curiosity about why they were veering from the quarry.

"Stay the course, son. Hold her nice and easy." It was a shame, Grogen decided, the veteran fighter didn't deserve what was coming, but he wasn't part of the team. Or the future.

Wondering briefly how it had all come to this, the SAD commander looked into the sideglass. One black GMC and one custom-built canvas-covered transport truck with government plates picked up the rear. It might be a strange and crazy world, one that was ruled by those sociopaths, but the cargo they carried—and that would stamp a gold seal on his own future—was something he could barely fathom.

Who could?

When first assigned to Area Zero he'd been briefed on what to believe. His Defense contract underscored the penalty for loose lips. They told him he would be burying nuclear waste and other toxins in the desert. They told him they were brewing a cutting edge rocket fuel in the underground labyrinth of the compound.

Whatever spent toxins resulted would be his task to secure and dispose of. They said they were creating nuclear propulsion from a toxin of unknown origin,
rumored to be capable of delivering man into deep
space at light speed. The source of the first batch of the
mystery toxin was so jealously guarded by Washington
that he was authorized to use deadly force if there was
even a whisper of a rumor that an employee at the compound even speculated about its origins.

The trouble was, no human tongue could ever really
keep a secret. Worse, when the hidden truth was sought
for personal gain, the future had a way of taking on a
life of its own, an angry leviathan boiling up from the
deep, ready to eat or be slain.

Another bounce through a deeper rut and Grogen
checked on the transport, his heart skipping a beat. Eight
fifty-five-gallon drums were encased in lead shields,
wrapped together with wire. The cargo was on steel pallets strapped to the walls. But he'd seen human flesh melt
inside HAZMAT suits from a spoonful's splash of the
mystery toxin. No way in hell did he want to be anywhere
near those drums when they were transferred. If it could
eat its way through material designed to see a man safely
through a few thousand degrees of nuclear fallout.

Grogen was shuddering at the image of the human
puddle when he spotted the behemoth parked on the
rise. Conklin looked at him when he said, "Flash your
lights, twice."

"Sir, I don't understand."

"You don't need to understand, soldier! Just do it."

Grogen felt the heat rise from his driver, but Conklin followed the order. The headlights on the eighteen-wheeler blinked in response. Grogen sighted two shadows on the port side.

"Park it, lights on. Fall out," Grogen ordered, slipping on his com link.

The driver was questioning the moment, reaching to open the door, when Grogen jammed the subgun's muzzled snout in his ribs. Hitting the trigger, Grogen blew him out of the vehicle and into the night.

Grogen saw armed shadows flapping their arms. They were shouting at one another in their guttural Brooklyn tongue, flinging around a variety of curses. He was out the door, subgun up, the transport rumbling up on his right flank when he spotted the red eyes dancing over his chest.

"Get those off me now, or the deal dies here!" he shouted. Another red dragon's eye stabbed the blackness from a jagged perch beyond the transport's cab. He marched on through the light, drawing a bead on the capo. "Do it!"

Advancing, Grogen felt his finger taking up slack on the trigger. His soldiers fell out, black-clad shadows taking cover behind the GMC and the transport. A quick count of hostiles, spotting two with AR-15 assault rifles hunkered behind the doors of an SUV, and he figured seven goons to his seasoned foursome.

"Everybody, cool it! Lose the light show!"

When the laser beams died, Grogen keyed his com link. "Road Warrior to Dragonship, come in."

"Dragonship here, sir."

"You have them painted?"

"That's affirmative, Road Warrior."

"Bring it on, but hold."

"Aye-aye, sir."

"You nuts, Grogen? What are ya doin'?" said the capo, approaching.

"Covering my assets, that's what." Grogen halted, lowered his weapon and studied the engineer of the future.

Mikey "The Pumpkin" Gagliano had broken out in a sweat. He swore as he noticed the corpse dumped by the Hummer and fired off more questions, lacing them all with the "f" word as if he'd invented it.

"Don't worry about it," Grogen told him as he made out the first faint buzz of rotor blades to the southeast. "You have my money?"

He waited for Gagliano to make the move, wondering how the capo got his nickname. Figure the fat head with cauliflower ears, a squat walrus frame with a buffet of pasta for a midsection had helped earn him the tag. The capo wasn't exactly dressed for warfare of any kind, standing there in his silk threads, Italian loafers and five pounds of gold. Typical hood. It was hard for Grogen to believe this was the future of the New York Mob, but the ilk of the Mafia lineage was little more than a long succession of thugs with a lust for money, power and pleasure. Brute animals, more hyena than lion, but still dangerous criminal scum.

"Joey! Bring the case!" the capo ordered.

Gagliano was on the verge of composing himself, squaring his shoulders, face hardening to street tough, when the rotor wash blew a squall over the rise. The hoods were shouting and cursing once again and Grogen was smiling as The Pumpkin jacked up the decibels of outrage at the sight of the winged behemoth.

"You wanna explain what's goin' on with that kind of firepower? I thought we had a deal, Grogen, but I'm startin' to feel you're ready to break it off in my ass."

"You just worry about me and my money," Grogen shouted back.

The capo was unable to take his eyes off the black warbird. It was a fearsome sight, and Grogen completely understood his anxiety. Hovering to the rear of Gagliano's SUV, Dragonship was a hybrid cross between the Apache and the Black Hawk. Winged pylons housed ten Hellfire rockets. Grogen knew a 30 mm chain gun in the nose turret was ready to cut loose on his word and grind them into puddles of human pasta and marinara.

Grogen grabbed the briefcase from Gagliano's errand boy and hefted it. "Something tells me you couldn't exactly pack two million in this," he shouted.

"You get the balance when I deliver the merchandise."

"That wasn't the deal."

"Neither was your messenger boy tellin' me to bring space suits if we wanted to check what we're buyin'."

"What you're buying, pal, isn't any tub of irradiated water."

"So you better be right."

"Heads up," Grogen called to his men. He tossed the briefcase toward the GMC. "Oh, I'm right, Mikey. I'm so right, if the people you're unloading it to get popped and start singing to the Feds like your boy back home we'll all be on death row faster than you can suck down a plate of linguini."

Grogen watched the fear flicker in Gagliano's cunning eyes. Thugs. Animals. Sociopaths. To do business with such loathsome creatures stung his professional pride.

What had started as his predecessor going for his own pot of gold now dumped Grogen into deep waters already chummed. And there were far bigger maneaters in this game than a bunch of leg-breaking hoods.

As Gagliano barked the order to roll the forklift down the ramp of the big rig's cargo hold, Grogen came to understand a little more about the future—what would separate the winners from losers. It all boiled down to survival of the fittest in his mind, but those without conscience or scruples held an edge. With what was on the table for the players in this future they would have to turn two blind eyes and harden the heart still more if they were to use the toxin the way he believed they would when it reached its principal buyer.

Grogen backed up, and his men moved away from the transport. He saw Gagliano making faces, holding out his arms.

"What the… You booby-trapped my merchandise?" The Pumpkin was startled.

Backpedaling farther from the truck, Grogen chuckled as he nodded at the forklift driver. "I'm merely establishing my comfort area, in case your driver tips it off the pallet."

Gagliano scowled and waddled away from the forklift. "You drop it, it's your ass!" he screamed at the driver.

"By the way, Mikey. There's been another change of plans," Grogen said, grinning.

"How come I know I ain't gonna like this already?"

"Your problem back home?"

"It's under control."

"Wrong. It's now under my control. See, you and me, Mikey, we're taking this ride to the end of the line."

"You don't trust us to fix the problem? You maybe worried about us stiffin' you on the rest of the money?"

Grogen smiled into the darkness. "No truer words have you ever spoken."

When United States Department of Justice Special Agent in Charge Thomas Peary considered the stats he reached the same conclusion he had during his first five years on the job.

The future of America belonged to the criminal.

Why bother fighting at all? he wondered. Once upon a time he'd been a devout Catholic, a family guy even, but reality had a strange and uneasy way of making a man a staunch believer only in number one. If there was a God, he thought, he was surely looking away from a world gone mad. Let the wild beasts eat one another.

Peary had problems of his own to solve, and the first of several solutions was sitting right under his roof. Soon, he would be packing up, moving on to a paradise of his own making and choosing. It might as well already be written in stone.

Peary was at the kitchen table, thinking about the culture of crime, when the future downfall of the New York Mafia fell into the late-night routine. Peary nearly bit his cigarette in two when the first chords of the same song he heard every night on VH1 videos blasted from the living room. By now he knew the lineup of hits by heart and had heard the songs repeated so many times the past week that he thought he might go ballistic any moment.

And, of course, every time a favorite was aired Jimmy "The Butcher" Marelli had to crank up the volume until it shook the floor and the walls of the Catskill hunting lodge.

Peary looked at the slab of human veal perched on the edge of the couch. His superiors claimed Marelli was last of the old school Mafia, honor among thieves and all that nonsense. He was a dinosaur among the new coke-sniffing crowd of backshooters and Mob clowns who killed while driving past sidewalk crowds, indiscriminately blasting any and everybody as long as they got their target. A button man who did his work one on one, face-to-face for the Cabriano Family. The Butcher was famous for whacking malcontents, traitors and songbirds, loyal only to the late Don Michael Cabriano. Only what Jimbo purportedly so loathed way back when he had now become.

The Mob was notoriously creative when it came to weaving legends about their own and making myth stick as truth for wise guy, public and G-man consumption. In this instance, the Justice Department had flown Marelli up the flagpole as a marquee hitter with a body count of biblical proportions to his credit. Whether or not that was true, Peary figured the hit man was costing the Justice Department a small fortune in wine and Scotch, cigars and cannoli alone. Not to mention all the veal linguini in white clams and twenty other pasta dishes he concocted and ate around the clock.

How many bodies, Peary wondered, really came attached to this baby-sitting detail on the government's tab? There were fifty-two kills the FBI and Justice knew about. The Butcher confirmed that during an eighteen-hour Q and A session. All the I's were dotted, T's crossed on the Who's Who of Mafiadom during his three decades of slaughter. There were at least two to twenty other corpses they were guessing had his brand on them, maybe more. Only Marelli enjoyed playing the big shot, stringing them along, feeding them just enough to have the FBI drag a river or dig up some earth in the New Jersey woods. Beyond cold-blooded murder he'd been granted full immunity for extortion, truck hijacking, assault, assault with intent, pimping, pandering and drug trafficking. There was also witness intimidation, tampering and execution. The deal was enough to make Peary wonder if the Justice Department had watched its balls go out the door with the change in administration, but he'd made his own plans well in advance to castrate the whole bull. The time to act, and get the hell out, had just about arrived.

Shaking his head, Peary watched the hit man, decked out in a flaming Hawaiian shirt and white silk slacks, staring dumbly at the blaring television. He wondered what the world was coming to. He was getting sick of being forced to breathe the same air as the pampered killer.

Suddenly Peary felt his hand inch toward his shoulder-holstered USP Expert .45. Ten hollowpoints in the clip, and a nasty little resolution to the noise problem flamed to mind.

"Sir? It's your move."

Peary laid an angry eye on Hobbs. The pink-faced kid was maybe two years out of Quantico, attached to the task force at the last moment when some desk-lifer at the FBI had, for reasons unknown, been able to catch and burn up the ear of the Attorney General. FBI, Justice, U.S. Marshals, everybody wanted in on this gig. It was a chance, he figured, a trophy for someone's mantel on the climb up the pecking order. Problem was, all the headshed wanted to do was make sure The Butcher was coddled and comfortable, practically warning them all to be careful not to upset or press him too much for information on the Cabriano Family. What next? Bring on the strippers? Everybody chip in for the guy's lap dance? All the big consideration and fawning the murdering asshole got, what happened to paying for your crimes?

Peary watched the FBI rookie shrink into himself under his steely gaze, then checked the board. Backgammon was the game, and they were playing for a four-hour watch, thirty minutes per win. But the way Hobbs had been rolling double fives and sixes on a whim and bumping him all over the board the past two hours, Peary figured he owed the kid two weeks' worth of shift duty.

"With all due respect, you need to relax, sir. Don't let him get to you."

"What's that?"

The kid showed a weak smile. "It could be worse. It could be rap."

Peary hit the kid in the face with a fat cloud that could have choked half a city block.

Hobbs flapped a hand at the smoke, making a face like he would puke. He coughed for another moment, then said, "I mean, he's a thug, sir, and a pain in the ass, but he can cook."

"So, he can cook for the troops, Hobbs, that make him a goodfella to you?"

"Well, what I meant—"

"Let me tell you something, son. I operate on the general principle I don't know a damn thing about another human being until they show me some cards. Just because you're in love with his spaghetti and meatballs doesn't mean he's shown a damn thing to anybody. Let me tell you something else, junior. I'm not in this world to be popular or liked. Fact is, the more unpopular, the more disliked I am the better I stand in my eyes."

Hobbs cleared his throat, staring at the game. "With all due respect, sir, I think there's a lot of anger in you."

Peary bared his teeth at the kid, wondering if he was serious or being a smart-ass. He looked at the board while running a hand over the white bristles of a scalp furrowed in spots by some punk's bullets long ago. Double sixes might get him back in the game.

He was shaking the dice when Marelli shouted an order for somebody to grab him a bottle of red wine from the cellar and some more cannolis while they were at it. Peary looked at Grevey and Markinson, wondering who would make a move as butler or if they had enough pride not to kiss ass. To their credit, he found both marshals with their faces buried in newspapers. They glanced at each other from their stools at the kitchen counter, passing the telepathy for the other to go fetch. Peary heard the thunder of his heart in his ears, then The Butcher cranked the volume high enough to bring down an eagle soaring over Windham High Peak.

It was more than he could take. The kid had to have seen it coming, but Peary didn't give a damn if a missile plowed through the roof. He was up and marching, the .45 out, the kid bleating something in his slipstream. The marshals were dropping their papers now, jowls hanging, but Peary was already sweeping past them.

Marelli was squawking for someone to shake a leg, when Peary drew a bead on the giant screen TV. The peal of .45 wrath drowned out the shouting and cursing around him. Marelli leaped to his feet, dousing his flamingos and island girls with blood-red wine. Peary became even more enraged when he saw the picture still flickering behind the smoke and leaping sparks. One more hollowpoint did the trick.

For what seemed like an hour suspended in time, Peary savored the shock and bedlam. He found less than ten feet separated himself from The Butcher and considered ending it right there. Marelli was bellowing, but it was clear to Peary he didn't know whether to shit or go blind. The kid, the marshals and the other agents on sentry duty around the lodge were now swarming into the living room, hurling themselves into a buffer zone between him and the wise guy.

Peary wrenched himself free of someone's grasp. They were all shouting at him, arms flapping, hands grabbing whatever they could. Marelli was already launched into a stream of profanity, threats and outrage, interspersed with taking the Lord's name in vain, among other blasphemous obscenities. He might have turned his back on Church and God, but he itched to shoot the hood for blasphemy alone.

Peary heard them asking if he was nuts, what was wrong with him and so on. Turning away and heading for the door to grab some fresh air, he heard Marelli railing how he wanted a new and bigger television, and he wanted that lunatic bastard off his detail or he wasn't talking to nobody. Peary encountered a marshal with an AR-15 who shuffled out of his path, but stared at him like something that had just stepped off a UFO.

"What?" Peary shouted, holstering his weapon. "You never see a TV get shot before?"

Peary rolled outside, breathing in the clean, cool mountain air. Alone, he laughed at the chaos he heard still bringing down the roof. What a few of them in there didn't know was a lot, he thought.

Losing a television was soon to become the least of Marelli's woes.

PETER CABRIANO TOOK a look at the bloody mass of naked flesh hung up by bound hands on the car lift, and believed he could read the future.

The empire was either his to save, or his to watch go down in flames. That was the problem, he knew, with narcotics trafficking. It built kingdoms, but it also tore them down. For some time now, he'd been scrambling to avoid this day, branching out into other avenues for fast cash. But narcotics had been the Family's bread and butter since the early eighties, and without the Colombians there would be no promise now of steering the Family into other business ventures, which he knew were the wave of the future.

There was no time to dwell on rewards not yet earned; he needed quick solutions. One answer was already in the works, but where there was one loose tongue he feared a whole goddamn chorus of squealers was out there ready to bring the walls crashing down.

Even though his Italian loafers were covered in rubber galoshes, he veered away from the oil splotches, found a dry spot in the bay, stood and considered the dilemma while his two soldiers watched him, awaiting orders. He was forty-six years old, but with a lot of life to live, two young sons to think of bringing into the business and worlds still to conquer. The keys to the kingdom were recently handed to him after his father died behind bars in Sing Sing from testicular cancer and complications of syphilis. The death three years earlier of his younger brother had left him sole heir, and no man who considered himself a man ever let a sister anywhere near the handling of Family business. He wondered how the old man would take charge of the present crisis. Two things he knew for sure. One, the old man would never snitch. Two, he would take the fight to his enemies. Part of the problem was figuring out who his enemies were.

The fiasco, he realized, all began when Marelli got popped by the FBI. Or maybe it started before that. How in the world he let himself get talked into the purchase and sale of what came from a classified spook base in Nevada, and in whose hands it would end up....

So what, he decided, he loved money. The focus now needed to be put on what Marelli had on him.

Cabriano ran his hands over his cashmere coat, gauging the number Brutaglia and Marino had done on Marelli's lifelong friend. A mashed nose, both eyes swollen shut, blood streaming off his chin where his lips were split open like tomatoes.

"Bruno. Wake him up."

Cabriano took a step back as Marino hefted a large metal bucket and hurled the contents. The effect was instant and jolting. Cabriano listened to Berosa's startled cry echo through the empty garage, the man shuddering against the sudden ice water shower, eyes straining to open.

"The beating's as good as it's gonna get, Tony. Talk to me about Jimmy. You don't, I think you know what's coming." Cabriano listened as Berosa cursed, called him a punk. He chuckled and gave Brutaglia the nod. "You know, Tony," he said, as he saw Brutaglia lift the small propane torch from a work bench, then twist the knob, a tongue of blue flame leaping from the shadows,

"Jimmy, he figures he can just walk out on me, retire to a beach somewhere, the Feds throwing their arms around him. Maybe he thinks he's gonna land some big book-movie deal, be a big star, a bunch of Hollywood starlets giving him blow jobs around the clock, telling him how great he is. He thinks he's gonna rat me out, bring me down, I end up doing life like my father while he's living the good life."

"You're nothing like your father."

"Whatever you say, Tony. Maybe you're right, but if you are it's because my old man didn't have to worry about snakes like you. He surrounded himself with loyal soldiers, stand-up guys who would go the distance, piss on a Fed's shoe if they even glared their way. What the hell happened to you and Jimmy, huh? Even the young guys, they thought of you two as legends. I don't get it. How do guys your age end up with a coke habit, anyhow? All your experience and you two get careless, don't even know when the Feds have every inch of everything you own bugged."

"It wasn't the Feds who came to us. Way he told it, Jimmy went to them."

"Then why is Jimmy stabbing me in the fucking back?"

"Think about it. Your father, he would never have approved of who you're dealin' with, what you're prepared to help them do."

"It's business, Tony, business. My old man didn't care for dope either, but he didn't mind using coke money to build himself a hotel-casino, did he?"

"Different business."

"How?"

"You punk, you don't get it, you don't have any honor."

"You're telling me Jimmy got all bent out of shape because of my new business partners?"

"What you're planning...your father would have shot you himself."

Cabriano was growing weary of the insults. No matter what, he knew tough when he saw it. He could burn the nads off Berosa, but the man wasn't going to break. Besides, the old soldier knew he was dead already.

He saw Marino moving toward Berosa, waved him off. "I don't suppose you're gonna tell me where the disk is?"

Berosa laughed. "Why don't you ask Jimmy?"

"That's a good idea, Tony. See, what you don't know is before the sun comes up Jimmy's taking whatever his big dreams to hell with him. I've got people on the inside, Tony," he said, and saw the stare come back, cold but believing. "Yeah, there's still a few Feds walking around willing to take my money. I know exactly where Jimmy is. Seeing as how he wants to live out his golden years so bad, I'm thinking if I get my hands on him, put a little fire to his balls he'll take me by the hand and walk me straight to the disk. What you did, Tony, you just told me you two are the only ones in my house I had to worry about."

"You're a disgrace to your father's memory."

Cabriano snapped his fingers at Marino to give him

his .45. The old soldier was still cursing him when he took the big stainless-steel piece. Then Cabriano silenced the loose tongue with the first of three rounds through the face.

2

All the years the man in black had been in the killing business and the evil of the savage opposition never failed to amaze, sicken and anger.

Where it was all headed, whatever the fate of humankind, he couldn't say, nor he thought, was it his place to venture a guess. He was a soldier, from beginning to whatever his own end of the line. As such, he believed common sense, basic decency and having eyes to see and ears to hear, could read into the telltale signs, sift through all the deceit and schemes of the age, and figure out where and how bad it could all get. No matter what the spin or political correctness of the time, no matter how much money was tossed around to turn eyes blind, two and two still equaled four in his game. Yes, there were subtle forms of evil spawning across the land, luring the impressionable or the weak and naive who floundered on the fence toward the abyss. But it was the leviathans of terrorism, international crime, mass murder and other forms of sabotage against the national security of the United States and the free world that was part and parcel of his War Everlasting.

Being only flesh and blood, there were days, however, he woke up and wondered how it had all come to this, where those in charge of running societies, those with power and money and the chance to make a real difference would have the world at large believe right was wrong, wrong was right, up was down and so forth. But they said the Devil was a liar, and his greatest lie was making man believe he didn't exist.

In the realm he walked it was clear a powerful force of darkness never slept. To him the laws of good and evil were as immutable and ironclad as Mother Nature. Up the stakes from murder of innocents by automatic weapons to weapons of mass destruction, morph a drug dealer or local hood into a dictator savaging his country in genocide, starvation and torture, and only the face of evil and the numbers of victims and depth of atrocity changed. Again, it wasn't his duty or destiny to be a preacher, politician, or Sunday-morning talking head. But there was clear and convincing evidence enough, from Baghdad to Bogotá to Beijing, that certain and many inhuman factors were hard at work on the planet to push the fate of humankind toward a point of no return.

For the man named Mack Bolan, also known as the Executioner, only a few good men and women rising up to tackle the extremes in action of the Seven Deadly Sins could somehow, someway, save the future, steer it all back on course before it was too late. Without question he counted himself among their ranks.

Big Tony's Used Foreign Imports was Bolan's launch pad for the new campaign. It was planted in a decent section of Brooklyn, a sprawling lot carved out between 6th and 7th Avenue, Prospect Park a short walk southeast. But the Cabriano Family hadn't seized their fortune on turning overpriced European wheels. For a moment, as the Executioner crouched behind the garbage bin at the end of the alley, the sound-suppressed Beretta 93-R out and waiting targets inside the garage, he felt a sense of déjà vu. A hundred lifetimes ago and too many ghosts of the good, bad and innocent to count, the soldier had taken on the Mafia. Back then, he'd been a one-man army, waging war against an invisible empire, at first striking down la Cosa Nostra out of a blood debt owed to his family.

Gradually, as the enemy body count grew, he came to see the true scourge of evil that was the Mob. These men who spoke of honor and respect and loyalty, even attended church—baptisms and marriages before the priest—corrupted everyone they touched, consumed every life that stood in their way to grabbing more profit, more power on the blood and terror of others. Back then it was gambling, prostitution, drugs, murder for hire, bribery, the usual list of sins. Over the years, between his own war and the savaging of the Mob by the Justice Department, the Mafia had nearly been decapitated.

Nearly.

Like when throwing the light on cockroaches, they skittered underground in recent years, erecting legitimate businesses to clean dirty and blood money, sons of Dons and capos earning law and business degrees.

Armed with education, and with an eye toward the future, the inheritors reached out to incorporate other homegrown gangs of thugs into their ranks, being equal opportunity employers in the new politically correct age. They dealt in wholesale shipments of narcotics from Latin America drug cartels, joined hands with other criminal organizations as far away as Moscow, reaping a big fat buck the common denominator, one for all. At present, with the insatiable hunger for weapons by terrorists that could wipe out tens of thousands, the game had grown even more deadly serious.

That, Bolan knew, was pretty much the gist of Peter Cabriano's rise to power and present status on the bad-guy list. With his father having wasted away behind bars, a younger brother who was a criminal defense attorney, but died—irony or justice?—from a cocaine overdose, Cabriano was king of New York. And he was reaching out to some of America's worst enemies.

Bolan had reconned the lot and surrounding block, but searched the premises again. Three gunshots, muffled slightly by the brick wall, had rung out moments ago. Assuming Big Tony Berosa had gone to judgment, Bolan watched the side door open, disgorging the Don of the day. He could have taken both Cabriano and his wheelman right then, but the Executioner had plans for the Don's future.

Six to eight stops were mentally penciled in on the soldier's hit list. Depending on how each situation shaped up, who gave him answers to questions that had drawn him into this mission, and provided he was blessed by good fortune—meaning he lived through the first couple of rounds—Bolan intended to net and skin some of the biggest man-eaters in a terror triangle that was, in his mind, both long in coming, and rife with apocalyptic overtones.

Feeling the weight of the mammoth .44 Magnum Desert Eagle riding on his hip, the weapon shielded from the naked eye by his long, loose-fitting black nylon windbreaker, Bolan watched the wheelman hold the door for his boss. Seconds later, the engine gunned, and the Towncar was rolling off into the night.

No problem. Bolan had Cabriano covered. Likewise, the Don's home, pier, every business clear to his Grand Palace hotel-casino in Atlantic City was under the watchful eyes of official shadows, all of whom answered to the soldier.

Satisfied he was alone with two wise guys about to be burdened with disposal chores, Bolan checked his six. Clear down the alley, but he was mindful of roving blue-and-whites given the coming play. Inside his jacket pocket a thin wallet with credentials declared him as Special Agent Matthew Cooper of the United States Department of Justice. It would pass the smell test, but cops still didn't like any G-man rolling into their town, shooting up bad guys and blowing up their places of business.

Worst-case, a phone call would be placed to Washington. There, Bolan's long-time friend, Hal Brognola, could untangle any unforeseen red tape octopus. The big Fed was a high-ranking Justice official, but he also

ran the nation's ultracovert black ops agency known as
Stony Man Farm. He was also liaison to the President
of the United States, who green-lighted all Stony Man
action. And woe be unto the lawman, lawyer or politician who needed to take a call from the White House
if Bolan was not given free rein and full cooperation,
with no questions asked.

Bolan didn't have to wait long. The 1958 white
Cadillac convertible with shark fins and whitewalls was
bucked up against the back door to the garage. A squat
bulldog he knew from Justice intel as Bruno Marino
waddled through the door. The wise guy threw a look
toward the lot, down the alley in both directions, then
keyed open the trunk. Frank Brutaglia materialized
next, cursing Marino as he lugged the tarp-covered
cargo through the door in a fireman's carry. Brutaglia
was dumping the load in the trunk, both of them now
grumbling and griping about who would dig the hole,
when Bolan made his move. No tough guy farewell
line, the Executioner rolled out of the shadows, Beretta
up and chugging. The first 9 mm subsonic round cored
through the back of Marino's skull, Brutaglia yelping
as he was hit in the face by blood and muck. Dead-
weight was crashing into Brutaglia when Bolan
slammed the next bullet between his eyes. He made
quick work of putting them in their resting place, dumping them on top of Big Tony. It was a tight fit, but there
was still a lot to be said about trunk space in the old
classics.

The Executioner closed the lid on their coffin and

leathered the Beretta. Retreating, he checked the parking lot. Before coming in, the soldier had considered fixing the fleet of fancy wheels with plastic explosives, but just as quickly dismissed the idea. This was a commercial-residential neighborhood, and no one on the block needed to pay indirectly for the crimes of these savages by finding their homes and businesses pummeled and damaged by raining debris.

Melting into the deeper shadows of the alley, Bolan determined for all enemies concerned reality was only just beginning to heat up.

JIMMY MARELLI WAS seething. The image of what the G-man had done, the blatant disrespect shown him, still burned in his mind. A change of clothes, a double Dewar's or three, and the junior G-man kissing his ass all over the place and swearing he'd get a better TV did not calm the storm inside.

Marelli went to work on his fourth double and fired up a fresh Havana, since he'd chewed the end off the other one during a fifteen-minute tirade. As he blew his way on a thick cloud into the kitchen, he was thinking there was a time not too long ago, Fed or not, he would have beaten the G-man so bad he would have begged for death—take his mother, wife, sister, please, just stop the pain. They didn't call him The Butcher, he thought, because he worked in a meat-packing plant.

Where had the good old days gone? he wondered, hurling open the fridge, chucking rolls of salami, prosciutto and three kinds of cheese on the counter. He hated living in the past, but couldn't help wishing he could step back in time. Where a man's word, his honor, was his own blood. Where a man did what he said he was going to do. Where busting heads or smoking another wise guy—execution-style or shootout—was business. Not like these punk kids today, who enjoyed inflicting pain, but only when it was safe to do so, no threat of payback. Cops, judges, politicians could still be bought, sure, but these days there was no heart in the younger generation, no pride, no honor in even the handling of the easy end. Speaking of easy, they all wanted easy street, but didn't want to risk getting their hands dirty. They wanted the glory, make their bones and all, but the idea of being a bullet-eater—a survivor who could wear the wounds proud—had about as much appeal to them as rap music to a hillbilly.

Where, oh, where had the days of honor gone?

He knew. They died with the real Don. A bunch of punks who were more show than go had been weaseled into the crew by the kid. No dummy, Marelli saw the future. He was a frightening dinosaur to this new breed, still feared and respected maybe, but things had changed. And when the Old Man died he knew it was time to get out, before one of the youngbloods got popped by the Feds and he found himself filling the Don's cell. Or some psycho punk with no honor and looking to make a name for himself, walked up behind him and shot him in the head.

Go west then, he'd decided. And he wanted to believe it had been a chance meeting in Vegas. However, the

spook knew the kid was looking to go international
with guys that would make the World Trade Center suicide bombers look tame and sane by comparison. He
and Berosa had decided it was time to think about retire-
ment. A talk ensued, a deal was struck and the kid took
the bait. Problem was, the Feds seemed to know about
the spook deal even before it happened. Come to find
out the kid had been looking to engineer just such a deal
with the Colombians and their new Mideast pals. That's
when, Marelli thought, he'd seen the end coming, sure
a blade was poised to plunge between his shoulder
blades, the whole deal falling into place too easy, and
he never trusted easy. Pretty slick, then, putting every
shred of detail about the Cabriano Family's business, A
to Z, including the spook angle on disk, and shipping it
off where, if needed, it could prove his own life raft if
the whole goddamned immunity deal sank like the *Ti-
tanic*.

Muttering a stream of profanity, he began conjuring
up ways to get back at the G-man for the insult. Food, like
Scotch, cocaine or getting a backroom hummer from one
of the girls at the club, normally helped ease the tension,
crystalize his thoughts. A fat sub wasn't going to cut it.
First he went to work on the half-empty pot of marinara.
Setting another pot on the stove, turning the flame on low,
he emptied the marinara into the new pan. To think he'd
been cooking for these assholes galled him. Fuck 'em. If
they insisted and pleaded for his linguini and white clams,
however, he'd reconsider, only next time he'd flavor the
sauce with some less appetizing ingredients.

He tossed the empty pot into the sink and grinned at the clattering sound that echoed through the lodge. He was taking a slab of Italian sausage out of the fridge when he found he had company. It was one of the marshals, Gravy or Groovy or something, perching himself on a stool, smack in the doorway, laying the assault rifle across his lap. Like he was making a statement: Jimmy would have to politely excuse himself in order to get past. Was this just another disrespectful asshole move, or was it something else? Marelli wondered. Did the guy want conversation? Was he boxing him in the kitchen for a reason?

Marelli washed a thick cloud of cigar smoke over the guy. Taking a butcher knife, he began chopping up sausage on the cutting board. "What?" he growled. "You wanna shoot my sauce off the stove?"

"He shouldn't of done what he did, Jimmy. That's just between us, okay?"

Marelli stared at the guy, didn't trust something he read in the eyes. He'd been around the block too many times to buy into whatever the guy was selling. No matter how much he gave them, he knew he was still just a murdering scumbag to these guys, smart enough to know all about lines in the sand. He turned and dumped sausage into the pot, turning the flame a little higher. Why were the hairs on the back of his neck rising? Something felt all wrong.

"We'll get you a new TV."

"How about a VCR with that shake?"

Groovy nodded. "That can be arranged."

Marelli grunted, took the knife and sliced open a sub roll.

"Hey, that smells pretty good, Jimmy, whatever you're cooking."

Marelli snorted. "Tellin' me you want some?"

"If you think you can spare a plate."

"I'll see what I got."

THE CABRIANO GENTLEMAN'S club was called the Fireball. For Bolan's intent and purpose it couldn't have been more aptly named. Unlike Big Tony's, the beauty of it was that the building sat alone. Bolan briefly wondered how many city officials were greased to give the immediate area an urban facelift, meaning plenty of elbow room from the Fireball to other establishments.

According to Justice intel, a fair amount of dirty money passed through the back room for the daily count of proceeds from drugs, extortion and local bookies paying their tribute. Agent who had the strip joint under surveillance, inside and out, figured four to six playboy hoods had enticed the girls for some after-hours celebration. The big spenders were enjoying a few hours away from the wife and kids.

The Executioner was moving, north by northwest, ready to veer due west after this stop to the Don's pier on the East River. That's where the big money was counted, but Bolan figured to help himself to a nice war chest at the Fireball before raiding the bank by the water. Take the Mob's money, and more often than not that slammed them with far more impact than blowing away a few street soldiers. After getting a sitrep from his agents, Bolan knew Cabriano was making a pit stop of his own in Cobble Hill, mixing pleasure with the mistress before proceeding to the warehouse on the pier.

Time enough for Bolan to light another fire.

An HK MP-5 with attached sound suppressor hung from one shoulder and a nylon sack dangled from the other side as Bolan rolled out of the alley, Beretta at the ready. He would have picked the lock on the back-door exit to breach the way, but found a wise guy had practically opened the gate for him.

The beefy slab was jangling around about five pounds of gold chains, giving instructions to the girl as he put his hand on the top of her head. It would have been better for him if he'd taken her to some bushes or used a back seat. Animal instinct for more than pleasure sounded the alarm in his head next, as he looked up, his lips moving at the sight of an armed voyeur marching his way.

Bolan saw the man was ready to bark his indignation about the infringement, then his eyes widened, Bolan not much caring what he saw or thought in his final act of desperation. The mobster shoved the girl away and was clawing for his .45 when Bolan tapped the trigger on his Beretta. The man went down, a dark third eye in the forehead. Bolan aimed the sound-suppressed snout at the girl. Shaking from blond mane to high-heeled pumps, she started to plead for her life.

"Do not speak to anybody about what you saw here," Bolan said. "You never saw me."

She bobbed her head.

"If you do, I know where you live. Go."

She went, and the Executioner slid through the door, dragging the body in behind him. He homed in on the laughter and the rock music at the end of the corridor. Bolan stowed the Beretta and filled his hands with the MP-5. Intel had advised Bolan that the office was on the other side of the bar, which was in the middle of the room.

Bolan rolled out into the open and took in the sights on the march. Four big spenders and four party girls in all, they had the place to themselves. To his left, two men were at the far end of the bar, one playing grab ass with a brunette in a string bikini, the other with his face buried in a pile of coke. The blonde on his arm was nudging him to move over and laying on some sass. Off to Bolan's immediate right, there was a twinkle toes, back turned, hopping from foot to foot in a drunken jig. He was waving bills at a playmate on stage, who, at Bolan's first glance, appeared to have enough money shoved in both garter belts to balance California's budget. Number four was the music fan, off with another brunette, fanning the pages on the jukebox, punching in favorites he'd never hear. The young hoods of the new Cabriano generation had probably never heard of Frank Sinatra, but Bolan noted they, like many who had gone before them, still preferred big .45s.

Mr. Hands was the first one to notice the party crasher, losing the girl with a shove and a shout and reaching for his weapon. Bolan responded with a

3-round burst to the chest that blew the gangster off his stool.

Mr. Selfish pulled his face out of the powder long enough to take the next brief 9 mm stream, a rising burst up the spine that pinned him to the barfront before he crumpled in a boneless heap at the feet of the blonde. The after-hours girls were screaming now, but holding their ground. Bolan figured they knew the score, having romped with their playboys long enough to know their day would come, but that they weren't the targets.

It worked for Bolan.

Tracking on, the warrior hit Twinkle Toes in the sternum as he was digging out his gun. Twinkle Toes was airborne across the stage, gun and cash taking to the air, hammering into and bringing down the mirror when the Executioner finished Jukebox Hero. Another triple load of subsonic 9 mm rounds, this time through the ribs. The wise guy bounced off the jukebox to a spray of glass, and Bolan looked to the partition that separated the office from the games. On the march, he issued the same directive to the party girls as the one he'd encountered on the way in. They were moving out, when Bolan heard a voice he assumed belonged to Bennie Guardino, the club's manager, cry out from hiding, "I ain't armed! Goddammit, who are you? Whaddaya want?"

"You alone?"

"Yeah!"

"Step out, hands up."

A skinny figure in a white silk jacket with slicked back black hair stepped into view.

"In the office. Move," Bolan commanded.

The guy kept blubbering questions as Bolan spun him and marched him down the short hall. Inside the office the soldier found Bennie had the day's take piled on his desk. The open safe revealed more rubber-banded stacks of bills. Bolan figured his war chest would settle in at three, maybe four hundred large. Not bad for a few minutes of work. He was sure the Justice Department's Task Force on Organized Crime would appreciate the effort.

Bolan shoved Guardino toward his desk. "This is your lucky day, Bennie," he said. He took the sack and tossed it on top of the bills. "Fill it up. You get to live."

Guardino sounded a nervous laugh. "You know whose money this is, pal?"

"I do. And it's about more than just the money."

"Yeah, sure, whatever you say. Whatever bullshit gets you through the night, 'cause this is your last one."

Guardino began stuffing the money into the sack, pissing and moaning about the plunder the whole time. They really didn't get it, Bolan thought, but he didn't expect any other reaction.

The soldier had reached his own conclusion about the love of money long ago. Unless a man or woman was raising children, giving to charity or feeding or educating a village, how much money was ever enough? For the savages, the answer was obvious. For honest, hard-working folks, live right, and one's needs were always met. It was the wants that always got in the way, human nature being the one constant in life, and it always ended up with the same result.

Ashes in the mouth.

Bolan took and hung the sack over his shoulder, then palmed the cell phone from the desk and handed it to the hood. "You're about to have a fire, Bennie."

"What are you talkin' about, fire? I don't smell smoke."

Bolan waved with the subgun for Bennie to move out. "Check your watch. Fifteen minutes, not a second before, call your boss. Tell Cabriano his problems have only just begun. Got that?"

"Yeah, I got it. I also know you're a walking dead man."

Bolan nudged Guardino in the spine with his weapon, heading him out the door. "I've heard that before. But here I am."

The Executioner took the first thermite canister from the pocket of his windbreaker, armed and lobbed it into the office. He ordered Guardino to hustle out of there, unless he wanted to get barbecued. He pulled the pin on firebomb number two and tossed it behind the bar.

The club manager was squawking at the sight of the strewed corpses when the first explosion rocked the club. Guardino cut loose with a stream of profanity and threatening noise. A swift kick in the backside shut his mouth and got him moving for the exit. Number two blast, spewing its ravages of white phosphorous, hit Bolan's back as he trailed Guardino into the alley.

"Fifteen minutes, not a second before, Bennie," Bolan warned, checking his surroundings, finding he was all clear. "I might be watching you." The hood was ready to try to get the last word in, when the Executioner added, "That should be enough time for you to put together a story."

"What story? I'll just tell him the truth."

"That'll be the problem."

"I don't know what your game is…"

"Cabriano. The man's going to want to know why five of his soldiers are dead, his club's in a pile of ashes, his money's gone, and you're the only one left to tell the tale."

The look on Guardino's face told Bolan that he finally got it.

The Executioner left him standing there to ponder his future.

3

Peter Cabriano was in no mood for the bookkeeper's number-crunching routine much less wanting to hear the bottom line on what he owed the government. This was no time to give away the first crumb of the fruits of his labor—inherited or not—to those who could never walk in his shoes. Anybody not in his camp could go straight to hell.

The Don was in the upstairs office, watching his crew below on the warehouse floor as they loaded the plastic-wrapped bundles of currency on pallets. Working on a Scotch and Marlboro, he was in hope, albeit dim, the alcohol, smoke and sight of the month's offshore haul—slated for steel containers to be settled in the belly of the Colombian freighter, *El Diablo*—would smooth out the edges of his raw nerves. Fat chance any indulgence would work. The night was not shaping up to be a stellar success. On all fronts he was feeling burdened by impending disaster. An indefinable ghost of death and destruction was out there. Some bad players were circling like sharks, smelling blood.

His blood.

He knew it paid to be paranoid when a man was sitting on top of the world. The problem with being a winner was obvious, he thought. Between jealous rivals, the Feds—even his own shrill, nagging wife—there was always someone ready to chop him off at the ankles. All being king of the mountain meant was that it was a long, hard tumble to the bottom. And if he fell there would be no one there to help him stand.

Take Pauline, for starters, he thought. No matter how much money, how much jewelry, how many condos, how many vacations to the world's paradise hot spots he took her, it was never enough. All the high hard ones he drove her didn't count for much anymore either, not when she was braying all the time these days for something more permanent and long-term, as in life. Pretty much par for the course, as far as mistresses went, but lately she was getting more demanding, more contentious—more threatening. There was, however, an answer for that particular hemorrhoid, but the solution could see him splashed all over the gossip rags, the brunt of talking-head speculation for years to come, everyone waiting for the gavel to fall, the bars slamming behind him.

Of course, at the top of the list, no question, there was the Marelli problem. And the answer to that crisis, already in the works, could see more heat, more badges, more wiretaps, more armed shadows up his ass than he already had. Next, there was his new venture with the Colombians, a road map to the future of the Family he'd drawn up just before the old man kicked off. If he had trusted them during their narcotics transactions about as much as he would sleep with a cobra, the feeling that far worse treachery now stalked him from their end was tripled, since their joint business endeavor had expanded to a whole new horizon. Toss in the government's ongoing investigation into the Saudi partnership at the Grand Palace in Atlantic City, bring onboard intelligence operatives who gave a whole new and frightening meaning to the word spook, and he began to question both his sanity and wisdom in upping the ante to grow his kingdom into an international empire.

Cabriano gritted his teeth when he heard the final tally of how much of the casino's skim could actually be cleaned, as opposed to how much cash he would have to declare to Uncle Sam. Considering the present audit, or so the accountant more or less told him, it looked like he would have to pony up in the neighborhood of ten million and change to take some heat off the Grand Palace.

"Did you hear me? Do you understand?" the accountant was asking.

"Yeah, yeah, I heard you. The percentage you take from me, you ever have any good news, other than telling me I may end up like Al Capone?"

"Just stating the facts, Mr. Cabriano. Now the way I see it—"

The phone interrupted more bad news. Cabriano saw the accountant staring at the phone as if it were a land mine. Whoever was calling at that hour, he could fairly guess, wasn't calling just to check on his emotional well-being.

"Answer it," Cabriano snapped, then turned his back to watch his crew wrap the first pallet with thick plastic sheeting. Figure twenty million was ready to be shipped out, and he was wondering if the Colombians would accept the fact he had the government's cut to consider, but already knew they didn't want to hear about his tax woes. With those guys, if one dollar was not accounted for against the last shipment, they might reconsider how trustworthy he would prove in the coming deal with their Mideast connection.

"Who's this?"

Cabriano whirled at the note of panic, saw the accountant's already pale face turn another shade of white. The phone was trembling in his hand, and his eyes bugged behind the glasses.

"Who is it?" Cabriano barked, the guy sitting there, shaking his head, lips moving, but no sound coming out. "Gimme that!" he snarled, and snatched the phone from the accountant's hand. "Yeah!"

"I left Big Tony with some company. You'll find the three of them in the trunk of the Caddie, at the lot."

Cabriano didn't know the voice, but why should he? What he did recognize was the warning bells in his head that this was no social call. The voice on the other end was cold, lifeless, floating in his ear like a call from the bowels of hell.

"Who the fuck are you?"

"There's been a fire at your club, too."

"What are you…what kinda game are you playin', asshole?"

"No game. Bennie will fill you in on the details. At first count, I'd say he handed over almost four hundred thousand before I walked out. Not too shabby for some walking around money."

Cabriano heard his heart thunder in his ears. "What? He did what? You ripped me off? You listen to me, mother—"

"No, you listen, Petey. The night's still young. The old things are passing away."

Cabriano exploded, ranting and swearing at the phone for several moments before he realized he was screaming at a dead line. He slammed the phone back on the cradle. He was glaring at the accountant, reaching for his cell phone when it trilled. He looked at the caller ID on the miniscreen and answered.

"You got something to tell me?" he growled, listening as Guardino began bleating out the incredible story. One big, dark guy, armed to the teeth like something out of Delta Force had, according to Bennie, strolled into the Fireball and blown away five of their best soldiers. He heard about the money next, close to four hundred large. Guardino was swearing on his mother's soul the mystery badass left him no choice, pumping out the apologies in between catching his breath.

"My club, Bennie, you better damn well tell me it's still standing."

There was sputtering, Guardino making a gagging noise, then he blurted out the awful truth.

And Cabriano went cold inside. Say Guardino was telling the truth, and he would find out for himself later, then his world was being threatened like no gang war he'd ever heard of. Whoever the nameless hitter he was a professional, though Cabriano could not really define just what a professional was. The bastard was either lucky, nuts, stupid or a combination of all three. Clearly, though, he had more to fear now than just the Feds. He hadn't given the Colombians reason—yet—to want to send him a message, though he knew they were in town, keeping close tabs on his movements and business.

"Boss? You—you there?" Guardino asked.

"Where are you?"

"I am at Bleeney's. Shit, I needed a few stiff ones after—"

"Go home."

"What's that?"

"You got shit in your ears? Go home. Wait there. I will deal with you shortly."

Guardino was bleating how sorry he was again, but Cabriano cut him off. Let him sweat, and if his account didn't wash with what would be a full police investigation, complete with visits from detectives digging even deeper into his business…

He called Frankie "The Tube." Ten rings later, The Tube was growling into his ear about did he know what time it was. Cabriano told him to get his ass out of bed, go over to the lot and look inside the trunk of the Caddie. He punched off before his lieutenant could start asking a bunch of questions and ignored the worried look from his accountant as he blew through the door. At the edge of the catwalk, he hollered down, "Look alive!"

He was about to relate the possibility they might be hit when he glimpsed something blur on a flaming jagged line across the warehouse. Before he could determine its direction, Cabriano nearly jumped out of his cashmere coat when one of the pallets blossomed into a fireball.

PEARY KNEW THE FUTURE was now. There had been pressure enough on two fronts for some time, the Mob boss wanting it done one way, the spooks with other ideas. Since both sides simply wanted the disk first, Marelli dead second, he decided to split the difference, opting against waiting until the spook crew arrived, to go ahead and take matters into his own hands.

Meaning he'd do it his way. Either way he'd pick up his money from both ends.

He slipped on the black leather gloves and keyed open the trunk to his Crown Victoria. With a few deep intakes of the cold mountain air, and feeling the eyes of Markinson and Jenkins boring into the side of his head, he unzipped the nylon bag. The first backup piece he hauled out was a Ruger Mini-14. He handed the rifle and 20-shot box of .223 rounds to Markinson. The old U.S. M-1 carbine semiauto with 30-round box went to Jenkins. Peary took the Mossberg 500 shotgun for himself and racked home the first 12-gauge round. He glanced at those who had been selected along with him for the job. Their faces were nearly invisible in the darkness, but he could sense the raw anger and disdain over what they were about to do.

In life a man made choices along the way. Sometimes they were the wrong ones, but no human being,
he reasoned, got out of this world unscarred, claiming
a strain-free soul. Whatever his choices, a man accepted
the consequences of his actions. For the three of them
it was pretty much the usual transgressions that had
landed them in the Mob-spook abyss. Filmed while
cheating on the wife. Accepting bribes. Mounting gambling debts. And Markinson and Jenkins even had two
murders-for-hire under their belts. The confusing part
for Peary was how the spooks knew so much more
about them than Cabriano, but he figured Big Brother
worked in ways more mysterious than a pack of hood-
lums with all of maybe a couple of high school educa-
tions between them. It was as if the spooks knew long
ago this day was coming, had properly planned to pre-
vent what was for Marelli a piss poor performance.

And Peary had his own ace in the hole.

He looked at the lodge at the end of the dirt drive,
aware that everyone inside but Grevey was moments
away from being cashiered out. Riot gun in hand, leading his fellow assassins toward the lodge, Peary plucked
the TAC radio off his belt.

BOLAN KNEW THE Justice Department had its sights set
on the Cabriano–Cali Cartel connection for some time.
The government was sure New York's premier Mob
Family was soon to be so much bad folklore and sensational headlines when they netted the big croc. The
trouble was, the castle did not crumble with the arrest

of the Old Man, though a deal was offered to him by the government. Instead of burying their heads in the sand, hoping the Fed storm would miraculously blow past them, the crime Family grew stronger, bolder, more prosperous. Fate stepped in to save the younger generation, as Don Michael took all his secrets to the grave. No squealing, not rat deals for him, he went out the old-school way, tough and unrepentant to the bitter end, but Bolan would never give that type of adversary points for honor among thieves.

Bolan believed all good things did come to those with patience, and the time had arrived for the angels to call in the Cabriano–Cali—and now—Mideast marker. Yes, the opposition had built an empire, enjoyed for years now the fruits of evil labor, thumbing their noses at the Justice Department. Up to a point, he had to admit crime did pay—for the criminal—but its sweet taste always turned bitter in due course, and there was much truth in a man reaping what he sowed.

Tagging the freighter the "Devil" was something of a middle-finger salute by its lonesome, but somehow it filled the arrogance of their Pandora's box to the brim. Along the southbound course, before docking in Barranquilla, the cash was divvied up in Charleston, Miami, the Bahamas. There were cigarette boats and swift executive jets that would haul the dirty money to other ports and airfields. Fat six- and seven-figure deposits filled offshore accounts of fly-by-night shell companies. Surveillance showed—between the casino's skim, drug profits and about ten other deep wells of illicit gain—the bimonthly cash shipments settled in at around twenty million.

The government might be after Cabriano for tax evasion, but Big Brother was about to become the least of his headaches.

The Executioner jump-started the fireworks of round three with a blow to where it hurt Cabriano the most. The 40 mm fragmentation grenade from Bolan's M-203 launcher fixed to his M-16 impacted a pallet that sat by itself, midway across the warehouse floor. Thunder, fire and smoke pounded through two hoods in that direction, a rain of shredded bills fluttering to the floor behind their airborne path.

Roving surveillance by Brognola's stakeout team had informed him a five-man crew was hard at work at the witching hour, ready to move the gold mine south. As with their previous stateside trips, and on orders from Cabriano, the Colombian crew of *El Diablo* was put up in a safehouse in Brooklyn. Apparently the Don didn't like the Colombians looking over his shoulder when he was counting cash. Fine by Bolan.

He found the enemy numbers stated by Brognola's guys was on the money. Downrange, he glimpsed the duo of sailing thugs end their fight with a thud into the side of a steel container. He scanned on. Tracking his next opponent, as screaming and shouting echoed, the Executioner tagged the brute in the forklift. The hood was digging out his .45 when the warrior's 3-round burst of 5.56 mm lightning blew him out of his seat. Somewhere in the racket of men in panic, Bolan made out the tempest of cursing and bellowing from the catwalk. That would be the new Don, Bolan suspected, far more bent out of shape over the loss of money than dead soldiers. For the moment, he and the accountant would keep.

The last two hoods were scraping themselves off the floor, coughing their way out of the smoke. Their bells had been rung by the concussive force of the blast, and their hands shook as they grasped for holstered side arms. Bolan treated them both to a quick dusting, sweeping his autofire, left to right. They were hammering on their backs when Cabriano began winging bullets from a big pistol. Bolan veered behind a steel container as rounds screamed off concrete to his left.

There was a pause in return fire, and Bolan heard the Don and the accountant shouting at each other. He snapped the assault rifle around the corner. The men were in flight down the catwalk as Bolan hit the M-16's trigger. He blew in the window of the office behind them, jolting still more panic into their gait.

The Don's Towncar was parked out back for a quick getaway. Bolan knew a team of Justice agents was on standby, to secure the building. He left the other pallets of currency for the care of Brognola's people, as planned. On the march, as he saw Cabriano and his number cruncher descend the steps for the back corridor, Bolan keyed his com link to get a fix on the wheelman.

IT NEVER FAILED TO AMAZE him how they thought they were fooling somebody. He knew the warning signs, could actually see a hit coming before it happened. Of course, experience did count for something—which meant surviving. Marelli briefly recalled how, four times in his day as a hitter, he'd been faced with similar circumstances. Sometimes they came smiling, but there was always a little wolf behind the look, like easy prey was on the menu, no sweat, party on the grave when the sure deed was done. Sometimes they were grim, too much so, telling him they weren't sure they had the stones or the talent to pull it off, worried as hell inside they might eat it instead, or worse, take humiliation beyond even the Devil's comprehension, forced to live with a memory worse than death. Then there were the cool ones, trying just a tad too hard to act naturally, foreplay before the high hard one, slicksters who'd seen one too many Eastwood movies but didn't understand one take was all they got in real time. Another category of type was shifty, the nervous ones, guys who practically shuddered up to the plate, waving their piece and hollering. In the end, though, beyond the types, it all boiled down to the same intent. Exactly where he belonged in the lineup he wasn't one-hundred-percent sure, but whatever he'd done over the years had worked. Figure acting was part of it, proper planning another, nerves of steel and will to do it yet another piece. Add being something of a student of human nature, reading the moment and measuring the mark, maybe catch him off guard or feeling a little too good about life, and the rare good ones could make it to double-digit hits.

Where Groovy landed was somewhere between cool and grim.

It just so happened Marelli found the marinara had come to a simmering bubble when the TAC radio crackled with Head Asshole's voice. He was slipping on the pot holder when he felt Groovy go as tight as a rising cobra.

"How you looking?" the voice sounded on the radio.

"Everything's beautiful in here, boss," Grevey answered.

A glance over his shoulder—Groovy was checking his watch, something from his boss about placing a bet on the Jets game this weekend, plus five—and Marelli knew it was on the way. Five seconds and counting, he figured.

The shotgun blast that came from somewhere around the corner, out in the living room, killed any doubt. Marelli was turning, pot in hand, Grevey rising, when staccato bursts of rifle fire added to his mounting fear. They were killing their own.

Marelli wasn't about to hang around and ask questions, aware he was the focus of the massacre. The marshal was lifting the rifle off his lap when Marelli hit him in the face with a scalding marinara shower. As Grevey screamed, the assault rifle flying up but cracking a round into the ceiling, Marelli followed up his attack, turning the bottom of the pot into a club. Cursing, he put 260 pounds of fear and fury behind the blow and slammed a home run, dead center in the marshal's face. It was the area he believed the police sketch artists called the triangle, just outside the eyebrows down to the mouth, where distinguishing facial characteristics defined one person from the next. One glance at the mashed and ruined mess that was the marshal, and Marelli knew that the man's own mother wouldn't recognize his face anymore.

Blood and marinara sprayed the air and counter like a burst fire hydrant, but Marelli forged into the gory rain, flinging the pot away to fill his hands with the dumped assault rifle. As the marshal bounced off the wall and slid down on his haunches, lights out, he considered putting a round through the marshal's brain, one less hassle to deal with.

Then the cavalry barreled around the corner.

IF NOT FOR THE DANGER of the moment, Bolan would have found the hasty flight slapstick comedy.

He saw the wheelman, .45 out and fanning the corridor, burst through the back door, when Cabriano bounded off the steps. Behind the Don, the accountant split the air with a shrill scream, spinning, this way and that, shielding his face and shoulders with a briefcase. The bookkeeper shimmied along in a sort of spastic tap dance, then stumbled and slammed into Cabriano's backside. As they went down in a tangled heap, Bolan hugged the corner of the wall and adjusted his aim. He tagged the wheelman with a 3-round stitching across the shins, dropping him flat on his back. The soldier was intent on sticking to the game plan.

Cabriano was cursing and triggering the .45 over the

accountant's head, the shots drowning out both sets of screams. Two wild rounds snapped past Bolan's ear, then the Don freed himself from the bookkeeper with a heel to his face. Cabriano lurched to his feet and cannoned another round over his shoulder. The wheelman was pleading for the Don's help, but Cabriano was clearly hell-bent on taking care of number one.

Which, in this instance, meant bolting out the back door, riding on.

Bolan let him run.

If Cabriano didn't believe it before, the Executioner knew he'd just made the Don fearfully aware the future was growing darker and more terrifying by the moment.

Soon Bolan would make certain Cabriano ran out of future altogether.

MARELLI FELT ELATED, even as he knew death was coming. All things considered it was better this way, he decided, more honor and respect, out from under their talons, able now to fight and die on his feet, or maybe somehow beat it out of there. Never again, though, to endure their disrespect, the sneers, the snubs. He was finished playing rat.

Instinct for survival, though, took over, as he backpedaled through the kitchen, capping off two quick rounds. The headcock, he was sure, could have sawed him in two with the big, nasty riot gun, but had opted to pull back behind the counter, cover himself from two more bullets chewing up the wall. With no spare clip, believing the mag he had in the assault rifle held twenty rounds tops, Marelli charged into the sitting room. One hand aiming the assault rifle at the doorway, he cupped a hand under the quarter-backrest of the heavy wood chair, spun and hurled it through the bay window. He knew it was roughly a ten-foot drop, with some bushes at the bottom to cushion his fall, but the ground then sloped hard, toward the woods. There would be rocks, vines and who knew what other potential bone breakers or flesh-eaters along the tumble. He glimpsed a few hanging shards of glass and cursed, but there was no choice. Unlike Hollywood, where the hero was always diving through windows getting nothing more than a few slivers in his coiffed do, he knew glass cut, and it could kill. He'd seen guys fall or get tossed through doors and windows more than once. They were lucky if they got piled onto a gurney for a hundred or so stitches.

Marelli crossed his arms over his face, snarled an oath, then ran and jumped.

"IF YOU HAVE SOMETHING for me, now's the time to save yourself."

Kicking the .45 out the door, as he heard the Towncar's engine gun, then tires squealing, the Executioner tuned out the whimpering of the accountant. He set sights and drew a bead with the M-16 on the wheelman.

"I talk…what do I get?"

"Another day, and maybe you keep your legs. Your choice."

"I wanna deal!"

"Not my call. Finishing you right now is."

The wheelman grimaced. "Okay, okay, goddammit! Marelli—he's gonna be hit. Tonight."

Bolan felt the ice ball lodge in his gut. "Keep talking."

"You don't know?"

"Know what?"

"You gotta be shittin' me. You ain't a Fed? You don't know? It's the Feds, the Justice Department. They're gonna whack Marelli for Cabriano."

Bolan felt his heart skip a beat. The world wanted to spin off its axis, but the soldier was out the door in two strides, leaving the hood to bleat at empty air about his deal.

"MARELLI! LISTEN TO ME! All we want is the disk! You come back, tell us where it is, you walk!"

Peary crouched beside the shattered remnants of the bay window, shotgun fanning the darkness. Markinson and Jenkins were on the other side, weapons ready, but he'd given them the order to hold their fire, even if Marelli opened up. He hoped the hit man did just that, muzzle-flash lighting up his position. He waited, straining his ears for any sound in the woods, cursing the silence. No rustle of clothing on brush, no twigs snapping, no sound of an angry, frightened man on the move, grunting and cursing his way deeper into the night. Nothing. Not even an angry reply from the hit man as he would have expected, given the situation and the guy's love of cursing. The fat bastard had just seemed to vanish into the night.

"We have to go out there and get him," Jenkins said.

"I know goddamn well what we have to do," Peary growled.

It was the worst of all possible worlds. Sure, they could stage the murders to look like a Mob hit, throw some shots in the walls and furniture, ditch the backup weapons in a lake, as planned. Grevey being down with a face like ground beef could help build the smoke screen: Marelli lashing out in a panic, making his break for freedom, fearing for his life. Mob hits were notoriously messy anyway, and the scene in the living room and just out front was one for a gangster's scrapbook.

Peary was shifting through plans A and B, deciding on his next call. Talk about falling into a pit, he thought. The list of those he would have to answer—lie—to could fill half a phone book. The big Fed in Washington for starters. But he was part of Plan B, so it all might work out yet. Then there was Cabriano, the spooks, all of them sure to get riled up that he'd taken matters into his own hands. Which could well mean a long delay in getting paid.

"These hills are covered with lodges, diners, little one-horse towns. He makes a phone…"

Peary gritted his teeth and hung his head. He didn't need Jenkins to remind him that Marelli reaching even a remote outpost of civilization could seal their doom.

"Marelli!" Peary shouted into the black hole that had swallowed up their songbird. "Last chance. You have two minutes to get your ass back here! You make us come and get you, I'll hand you over to Cabriano myself!"

Silence.

"Okay," he told Markinson and Jenkins. "We do it the hard way. Get the night-vision goggles, break out the map."

"What about Grevey?" Jenkins wanted to know.

"What about him?"

"He needs a doctor."

"Screw that noise. Wake him up."

Peary gave it a few more moments, hoping Marelli would take the bait, but knew the guy was way too savvy—and now armed and dangerous, a rabid beast on the run—to just stroll back, all's forgiven. He was pacing when the cell phone with secured line trilled on his belt. One look at the caller ID, and he felt his heart race.

"I can't believe it," Peary rasped, but punched on. "Yeah."

And heard Don Cabriano ask, "Is it done?"

4

Hal Brognola feared for the future of the so-called free world. Beyond the West and its often unfaithful, disloyal, fly-by-night bedmates, there was, of course, the sum total of humanity—six to seven billion people—to consider. No paranoid xenophobe or raving jingoist, he was a realist, a staunch old-school believer in the black and white of right and wrong. That in mind, he was aware that he had not made the rules of how the drama of the bigger picture was played out, but believed, for better or worse, as freedom in the West went so did the rest of the world.

Sad perhaps, but true.

Not only was he a high-ranking official for the U.S. Department of Justice, but he was in charge of the "unofficial" ultra-covert Stony Man Farm. As such, between the double duties of protecting America's national security, he had access to the kind of intelligence—sometimes stolen from cyberspace by the computer team at the Farm—that reached only the President's desk. And, as such, he not only stayed informed—up to the second on flashpoints and epicenters of critical mass around the globe—but could read developing and frightening trends.

Case in point, he thought, was the last of the big-time crime Families in New York. And the Cabriano Family and its latest playmates on the world stage were the reason he was driving into Arlington for a predawn meet with those who probably had access to more intelligence…well, in their eyes, he considered it probably put them one step beneath the Almighty.

Lack of sleep, too much coffee and too many antacid tablets had his mind racing. He tried to pull his thoughts together, focus on the task at hand, but found it hard labor at the moment. A man with the weight of the world on his shoulders once again, eyes that saw and ears that heard, he figured the mind tended to jump around.

He'd been there before, more times than he could count.

And if what he knew about the situation in New York was even half-true, then God help the human race.

Brognola passed a white county cruiser rolling the opposite direction, two more vehicles trailing the policeman to a stop sign. Aware the working force of the town was coming to life, he was slightly annoyed he might have to fight traffic on his way back to his office, knowing the action would be heating up in New York, as it always did when Bolan set his sights on the enemy. Slowly driving past a bank, he spotted two more cruisers, parked side by side, window to window, in the parking lot. He was on the side of the law, but a fleeting sense of paranoia gave him pause. Given Bolan's current mission, the hanging questions, the dire outcome if the Cabriano Family succeeded in achieving its goals, he passed off his unease as a healthy sign his head was in the game.

This wasn't the first time he'd been sought out by intelligence operatives who had—or claimed to have—the facts of life on whatever the present critical mass. Information equaled wealth in his world, but there was something about the setup that wanted to bring the hammer down on the warning bell inside his head.

He was out there on the request of the assistant director of the department's Special Task Force on Organized Crime. The joint team of marshals, FBI and Justice agents sitting on Jimmy Marelli fell under Brognola's control, but Rollins had culled the eight-man detail himself, flexing bureaucratic muscle, rolling out the red tape, until Brognola put the brakes on the one-man show. Armed with the facts on Cabriano as he knew them, Brognola had stepped in, landed Bolan in charge of the operation, from Atlantic City to Brooklyn to the Catskills.

He recalled briefly the minor resistance Rollins had thrown up. The AD bowed out to put Special Agent Matt Cooper in charge only when Brognola had picked up the red phone in his office, inviting the man to interrupt the President's Herculean schedule.

Turning on the designated street, sticking to the AD's directions, he motored on, mentally playing back some of the last conversation with Rollins.

"I've been working certain sources of mine in the intelligence community, regarding the Cabriano–Cali Cartel–Mideast connection. They say they know where—how should I say—an advanced, highly volatile form of radioactive waste is being smuggled from. They claim to know who is responsible for helping Cabriano and the cartel in this new thing of theirs to sell the raw material for a dirty bomb, which, they claim, is composed of a toxin unlike anything science has ever heard of. Very nasty stuff, or so I'm told. For whatever reason, they requested they meet with you to pass on the details. It's your call, but I think it's critical you meet with them."

So be it. Call him curious or simply dedicated. Brognola accepted the midnight request.

Ahead, he spotted the tennis court, his landmark, as he rolled over the rise. Thinking about Bolan, the big Fed turned onto the cul-de-sac, slid up against the curb, parked and killed the engine. The AD informed him two spooks would be waiting for him in the park, on the far side of the court's mesh fencing. He sat, scanning the Stygian gloom of woods beyond the court. Brognola decided if they were out there they could wait, as he searched his windbreaker for the cell phone with secured line. Slowly—as he patted empty pockets, then found nothing clipped to his belt and swept the seat— it dawned on him he'd left his one source of communication at the office. He muttered an oath, angry with himself. The rare oversight heightened his sense of anxiety, an urgency mounting to conclude this meet and get in touch with Bolan.

Stepping out, Brognola checked his surroundings. He became aware suddenly of the weight of the Beretta 92-F, hung in the shoulder holster on his left side beneath his windbreaker. Somewhere an engine revved, a car door closed. Brognola's nerves were edging raw, as he looked in the direction of the sounds, then glanced over his shoulder at the suburban enclave ringing the dead-end street.

All by himself.

Deep breath, he thought. He was acting like a rookie, one day out of Quantico. Or was he? He'd been around, seen enough to trust his gut, so...

Brognola stepped down the grassy knoll, peering into the woods and brush fanning away from the court. He hated this clandestine business, marching into the unknown, always braced for the worst. But he had to admit in the past the intelligence he'd gained from such encounters far outweighed personal feelings.

Still...

Brognola thought he spotted a tall shadow, floating, it seemed, in the woods, twenty yards out. A few more steps, catching the movement of a silhouette to his left, and Brognola felt the hackles rise on the back of his neck. The gong was going off in his head, then he caught the sound of rustling to his right. His instinct—fight or flight—was split down the middle. Light was poor, at best, a few broken shafts hitting his back from the cul-de-sac dwellings.

What the hell was going on?

Brognola reached into his jacket, drew the Beretta,

thought he heard, then glimpsed darting movement going from his left to right. If they were there—and Rollins implied two spooks with no names—why the games?

He sidled off to his right, in the direction where he thought he spotted the last moving shadow, instinct telling him the area was vacated, his back clear. Brognola slowly turned the Beretta swinging around as he saw two tall shadows roll out from behind a stand of trees. He couldn't see their faces, but he made out the bulky shapes of large handguns as the weapons rose and drew a bead on his chest.

Brognola darted hard to the side, but knew it was too late to clear their line of fire. He heard the loud double crack split the darkness, a microsecond before he squeezed the Beretta's trigger, then felt the sledgehammer force of rounds impact flesh.

THE RECEPTION COMMITTEE Bolan found framed in the Bell JetRanger's spotlight did not belong to the task force under his command. As the Justice Department pilot lowered and angled the chopper toward the clearing beside the lodge he ordered for a landing zone, it became clear to Bolan his fears were justified. The mission was on the edge of going to hell. One look at the trio in blacksuits and com links, two wielding subguns and the odd man out toting a large combat shotgun, and the soldier could fairly assume they weren't park rangers or local ops. The ones standing were not his guys, but the two bodies he saw in front of the lodge beneath the white halo did belong to the task force.

What happened to his men—and to Marelli?

During the drive to Newark International, where Brognola had arranged a designated hangar with chopper and Gulfstream for the task force, Bolan had steeled himself for the worst. And the short chopper ride to the Blackhead Range Wild Forest Preserve in the Catskills had been time enough for the soldier to load himself down for all-out combat. Webbing and vest chocked and stocked with spare clips and a mixed assortment of flash-stun, incendiary and frag grenades, the soldier did not want to get caught short when it hit the fan. About to venture into the unknown, his main piece, an M-16/M-203 assault rifle combo, was in hand, with the HK subgun slung across his shoulder ready as backup. A commando dagger was sheathed on his shin in case all else failed.

Ready and set, but for what exactly?

That he had not been able to raise Brognola after four attempts only darkened the soldier's foreboding. Since the big Fed never strayed out of arm's reach or cell phone or satlink range when a mission was launched...

The chopper touched down. Bolan decided there was only one way to start getting answers. He was out the door, M-16 leading his march, when he sensed the armed shadows stiffen, then one mouthed what looked like an order to one of his men. Combat senses searing adrenaline through his veins, Bolan picked up the pace and lifted the M-16. Instinct took hold and veered him toward the cover of the task force's Crown Victoria. It hadn't escaped his prior observation that the other unmarked vehicle was missing, but the soldier was locked on the shadow sliding up the side of the GMC, the vehicle backed-in for obvious quick exit. Bolan was about to announce himself when he glimpsed the slender tube, up and aimed outside the door. The LAW was spitting its 66 mm HEAT round next, the missile wobbling on, whooshing past the soldier within arm's reach on a tail of smoke and flame; as the HK subguns cut loose, the shotgun thundered in sync.

Bolan hit the deck as glass blew over his head and a fireball erupted behind in a thunderclap, pounding him into earth with seismic shock waves.

EYES STUNG BY BLOOD, Brognola kept capping off rounds, bent on taking the bastards with him as he toppled. Sight and sound seemed to mesh with the fire racing through his body as reality fractured into a dreamy mist. Somewhere in the bellow of silent rage in his head, he knew he was dead on his feet, cursing Rollins, as he felt another round tear through his side. Shooting wild, he thought he heard a sharp grunt. He was still falling, it seemed, from a great height. Instinct, reflex and fury gripped Brognola, his head and shoulders slamming off a solid object, stars exploding in the sky. He heard the snap of bullets in his ears, slivers of something lashing his face. His finger kept hitting the trigger, the weapon taking on a life of its own as he sprayed rounds into the darkness.

He became aware that he was down, flat on his back. The angry life force inside seemed to roll him over, behind whatever he'd hammered against and was now shielding him from the barrage.

And Brognola heard the groan tear from his lips, hover next, it seemed, up there in the blackness. There was a rustling sound, drifting away, a blurred glimpse of a shadow in the night fleeing.

Brognola felt himself go utterly still, tasted the blood in his mouth. He listened to the rasping wheeze as it slowly began to fade away, the sky turning blacker. There was no rolling collage of the sum total of his life, but Brognola pictured his wife, thought about Bolan, then found it strange how the stars appeared to wink out, one by one.

SOMETIMES THE GODS of war intervened and helped those who were on the side of the angels. With the roar of the blast and the invisible hammer of shock waves, the Executioner felt superheated wind rush over his shaky cover. No time to consider his good fortune—another few yards closer to the fireball and he would have been incinerated—he glimpsed wreckage winging past the Crown Victoria.

And flying straight for the hardforce.

A jagged strip of rotor blade whirled for blacksuit and sidekick, their weapons going silent as they ducked the airborne guillotine.

And Bolan seized the lull to help himself.

Popping to his feet, the Executioner returned the explosive favor, triggering the M-203. Mr. LAW was chucking away the spent antitank launcher wheeling to run, and made it all of two lurching steps when the projectile slammed into the GMC's grille. He sailed away, blast and body appearing to be vacuumed through the obliterated bay window to the living room.

Gone and forgotten.

The blast had dumped the other blacksuits on the ground. One was howling mad as metallic flying piranhas fed on his carcass. He was hauling himself off the ground, bracing the barrage of fire and brimstone, bringing the combat shotgun to bear when Bolan blew him off his feet with a 3-round poleax to the chest.

With a good idea of who the opposition was, Bolan moved toward the lodge. Closing in, he found the third blacksuit was missing part of his skull, half his face sheared to the bone. Whichever blast sealed the deed, his brains now dribbled out, one eye fixed on eternity.

The Executioner watched the doorway, looked into the living room, strained to hear through the twin crackle of bonfires for any sound that other blacksuits were on the loose. He would check, of course, but sensed the utter stillness of death, inside and out.

Beyond cold anger, the soldier knew his problems had only just begun. The lodge, he knew, had been used to house federal witnesses before Marelli. It had been selected for its remoteness from campgrounds, hikers, Park Service, with a NO TRESPASSING-GOVERNMENT PROPERTY sign posted at the end of the dirt drive. Bolan knew the lay of the land from a previous trip and a recon of the area in question. Something like eleven thousand acres of dense forest and rugged hills surrounded the lodge in the Blackhead Range. Tucked between Lake Capra and Black Dome, he knew the nearest campground, lean-to or hiking trail was miles away in any direction. Same for any Park Service outpost.

A quick backtrack to the Crown Vic, finding keys in the ignition, and the soldier knew, providing luck held, he could beat any wandering officialdom out of there.

Bolan stole a moment to look back at the funeral pyre in the clearing. Traitors walked among the ranks, but the Executioner would hunt them down. There was no place for the animals to run or hide. Make no mistake, there would be an answer for this treachery.

There was no time now to grieve for the Justice pilot or curse that his satlink and cell phone with secured line went with the man. Bolan was alone, cut off from the world, walking among the hyenas. So be it.

Near the front of the lodge, Bolan looked at his two murdered agents and vowed to himself their deaths would not be in vain. Next a frisk of the two blacksuits found no identification. The Executioner ventured into what he already knew was a charnel house.

BROGNOLA COULDN'T SAY if he walked or floated toward the light. He vaguely recognized a voice as his own, just on the edges of the ringing. The rasping in his ears told him to keep going.

He was still on the planet.

There was a gradual awareness of a burning sensation all over, mounting in anger, it seemed, the closer he drew to the light. There were indistinct shadows in the light, he believed, evanescent then in the white shroud as he felt blood and sweat burn into his eyes. Were those voices he heard? Were those faces, mouths open, shouting?

They were spinning angry demon faces, Brognola feeling tugged on by their presence, a shadow of instinct telling him what they were, that he was plodding toward his car.

"Drop the weapon!"

Cops, he thought. He believed he said "Brognola. Justice Department."

Then the darkness came once more to take him away.

FOUR DOWN, FOUR GONE, and no Marelli.

As he listened to the hungry flames eating away beyond the door, Bolan knelt beside the last body. Hobbs. Young guy, he thought, virtually no experience. Handpicked, the soldier suspected, for the slaughter. Bolan had only met him the one time he was briefing the task force. More life, another promising future brutally snatched away by the evil of other men. The soldier couldn't say if Hobbs had family, but had to believe there would be grief enough to go around when the word of his murder reached home.

Brushing shut those young lifeless eyes, Bolan pondered the scene, the dilemma. A thorough walk-through of lodge and perimeter, covering every foot and every nook and cranny of the building, Bolan could pretty much picture what happened. The dead agents never knew what hit them. A check of their weapons showed they had capped off plenty of rounds, but the way the walls were scarred, the furniture shot up, it was overplay for the staging of the crime scene. Figure Peary and his jackals had cut down the others in seconds with backup hardware, hands gloved, then borrowed their weapons to shoot up the place. A phantom firefight. He wondered exactly how the traitors planned to dig themselves out of this pit. They were in it for the money, most likely, corralled by Cabriano or maybe the blacksuits for the job or both. Figure the transgressions of Peary and the others were used for blackmail. Good guys gone bad, Bolan knew, could prove the most dangerous animals.

Marelli, it appeared, had been in the kitchen, whipping up a hot meal. Whoever took the marinara facial on the stool, the imprint in the bottom of the pot could get a police sketch artist started on bringing the perp to picture. One of them, at least, was wearing his shame, ruing the night. Small comfort in light of the fact Bolan figured at least three packs of savages—between the Mob, the blacksuits and the traitor foursome—were on the prowl. Whoever the blacksuits—figure NSA, DIA or some black ops arm of DOD—they added a new wrinkle. If there were more of them in the Catskills or on the way to beef up the first group, Bolan knew they would be armed with high-tech tracking, surveillance and countersurveillance that could rival anything he was equipped with.

And the blacksuits, he knew from his briefing with Brognola, were part of the bigger, nastier picture. The big Fed suspected, but couldn't prove, radioactive waste was being sold to Cabriano from traitors on the home team. From there it was, allegedly, going to be handed over to the Cali Cartel, who intended to turn around and unload it to an unknown group of Mideast terrorists.

Marelli was the key. The hit man claimed to have the facts of life on the Cabriano Family, the cartel and the skinny on the blacksuit-radioactive-waste angle, all on a disk he had squirreled away, his ace in the hole. Well, the hit man was right then running scared, alone, hunted by Peary. Bolan guessed Marelli was armed, grabbing whatever weapon from the agent now walking around in search of a plastic surgeon. A chair through the bay window, and Marelli would be down the slope, into the woods.

And Bolan knew they were some big woods.

The hit man's escape route would be south. Bolan pictured the lay of the land from prior foot and aerial surveillance. Two narrow serpentine dirt roads ran north to south, leading toward the Colgate Lake Trail. No reason to assume Marelli had a clue what was out there. He could wander for miles in any direction before he reached anyone or anything to help him. Marelli was every bit hung out there by himself, Bolan knew, as he was at the moment. Forget calling any pals in New York City, Cabriano had probably offered a nice chunk of change for The Butcher's head on a pike.

As far as Bolan was concerned, the only one he intended to keep breathing was the hit man.

The Executioner offered a final thought for the slain agents and loved ones left behind.

Then he rose and walked out the door.

5

It boggled the mind.

The mobster, he thought, was a city slug, five-and-a-half feet, packing an extra sixty to seventy pounds of suet. The closest he probably ever got to country was somewhere out in the Jersey woods to bury a stiff. God only knew the tonnage of cannolis, calamari and pasta devoured, all the Scotch and red wine that swelled ample belly, ate up brain cells, all the acreage of tobacco smoked over five-plus decades. Talk about a walking toxic waste dump. And he was decked out in aloha shirt and slacks whiter than pure ivory that would have dimmed the sun in comparison. Peary thought it should have been as simple as strolling out of the lodge to pick up the trail. Practically bathed in pungent aftershave on top of it all, there was also the soft leather of Italian loafers, hardly footwear suitable to absorb a hard double-time over ground studded with rock and twigs. The unrelenting turf should have resulted in an angry yelp, a curse, anything.

But there they were, traipsing through the forest, spread out at roughly fifty foot intervals, east to west, moving north, hoping to intercept Marelli in light of his original running point. Not a sound so far, no whiff of poisons or cologne, not a fleeting glimmer of the guy in the green hue of NVD headwear.

It was like the mothership came down and beamed him up.

Peary maneuvered his way through the forest, avoiding tangled brush. Searching for a footpath, Mossberg out and fanning, he heard a sudden snap. Jolted, he pivoted, found only Jenkins to his far right, blundering through some brush, muttering an oath. Great, he thought, the slug was apparently escaping, as silent as a ghost, and his guys were showing all the stealth hunting skills of a T-Rex on the rampage.

According to his watch, daybreak was an hour or so away, but the birds were already out, chirping and squawking, helping to muffle the slightest indicator Marelli was in the neighborhood.

Bad news had already hit the other concerned parties at bullet speed, leaving Peary to anxiously ponder how much worse things could get. After the verbal flogging by Cabriano, then getting his ear burned up by the spook—and where had those bastards come from anyway, much less gotten their TAC frequency?—he'd ordered his men to turn off TAC radios and cell phones, stick to com links and break radio silence for an emergency or a Marelli sighting only. Yet two more hassles, tightening the noose. Say Cabriano and the spooks decided he couldn't turn the crisis around, the Catskills could find an army of shooters in the area by sunrise.

He could hear the blame game in his head already, the threatening noise about dereliction of duty, that maybe he was getting paid too much, and for a simple job a greenhorn hit man could have done for half the price.

"Son of a—"

It was obvious, too, Grevey needed medical attention. Beyond the nose mashed into his face, the man's lips were split to the bone, his jaw was broken and his eyes were swelling shut. When they ditched the Crown Victoria on the dirt track, Peary briefly recalled how Grevey could barely manage to stay on his feet, wobbling off into the forest, making all kinds of racket. But there was nothing Peary, or any of them could do, but keep going, find the porker before he stumbled across another human being, thus breaking the news, turning wilderness into an armed camp of cops and God only knew who else.

Then there was the real SAC of the operation to worry about. Some Super Agent dumped in their laps at the last minute. The big guy named Cooper was something of a mystery. The whispers around the Justice Department were he was more than just a run-of-the-mill G-man. What he was exactly—the floating rumor was military—no one knew, or was saying. At present, he was somewhere in Brooklyn, or so Peary hoped. Doing what, he couldn't say, but most likely causing Cabriano grief. From the ranting and raving on Cabriano's end it sounded like the crime boss was under siege, businesses getting torched, soldiers shot up under his nose. A big, dark guy, the Don claimed, one man armed with enough firepower to field a squad of Green Berets, was burning down the kingdom.

Assuming the worst, that would be this Cooper character. Whatever he was, orders from above were to grant him carte blanche. The good news on that front, however, was the fates of two men deemed enemies to the cause were in the process of finding the stone rolled over their tombs.

Peary stumbled over a large rock and bit down a curse. Suddenly, he heard Markinson patching through, and keyed his com link. "What?"

"You need to get over here."

Peary caught the anxiety in Markinson's voice and felt his anger rising, wondering why the man just didn't spit out the problem. "What is it?"

"You need to see this."

"Goddammit, just tell me."

He balked, eyes darting around the woods as the snarled words echoed into the dark.

"It's Grevey. He's dead."

MARELLI WAS SURPRISED at how quick and quiet he moved through the forest. Fear and adrenaline, though, could work magic, he figured, lighten any load under duress. Still, he knew he was in no shape to keep up the hard jaunt much longer. Even considering he was being hunted like an animal for slaughter, years of indulging every whim and vice would soon take its toll, like a tire with a slow leak.

In fact, he was already sucking wind, limbs ballooning with sludge, stomach churning with bile, cannoli and wine squirting acid residue up his throat. His clothing—ripped at the knees from his roll down the slope, a gash on his shoulder where glass tore him on the way out the window—was plastered to flesh running with sweat mingled with blood. The soft shoes didn't help cut back on the grief either. Every stone, root, piece of hard vegetation jabbed into his toes, the balls of his feet. The heels, fiery daggers, it seemed, sliced clear to his pulsing brain. For once in his life, though, he kept his mouth shut, but silently cursed every tortured step.

Damn, but he needed a smoke, a drink. His mind was screaming at him to stop for a rest. He knew if he sat still for a moment, though, his pursuers would gain ground. That, and he might be tempted to stop running altogether, consider handing himself back...

No way.

As soon as they broke him—and he was sure torture was on their play card—he was finished. Cabriano or the federal sharks, dead was dead, once they got the disk.

He thought he heard them, somewhere in the distance. Was that a curse? How close were they? Could they see him? Beyond fading moon and starlight, with the gray wash of predawn fanning over the forest rooftop, there was barely enough light to make out the black sentinels of trees, avoid a header over ground broken in spots, a swan dive into a ravine. No clue where he was headed, he believed a New York cabbie would know way more about hiking through the forest than he did.

How long had he been running? An hour? Ninety minutes? Two hours? Did it matter? And what would he do if he came across a camper, hiker? With luck, he'd stumble into someone with wheels. A carjacking was the least of his concerns, since it sure looked like any deal of immunity was down the toilet. In fact, he could imagine his hunters hanging the murders of their own on his scalp.

Marelli wandered to the edge of the tree line and stopped. With a long look over his shoulder, he listened to the dawn racket of birds swarming overhead. He considered checking the clip, but knew there was no time to pop out rounds for a tally. Call it thirteen to fifteen shots, and he'd make every one of them count.

He looked across the clearing, figured a twenty-yard dash to the other side before he could slip into still more dense forest. Keep going, he told himself, luck had to be on his side or he wouldn't have made it this far.

Another hard search to calm his fear, he was about to move out when the bile shot like a flaming sword inside his chest. Gagging, he dropped to one knee, choking back the slime, cursing himself to pull it together, keep quiet. A few moments later, the sickness faded. Hand braced on a tree, he was rising when he felt cold metal dig into the base of his skull. He froze.

"At this very moment, I'm your only shot at salvation."

Marelli thought he should have recognized the voice, but couldn't place it, only knew it didn't belong to any of the marshals. His gut warned him that whoever the phantom was, this voice from the bottom of a tomb was giving him a choice, but would just as soon kill him as save him.

THE MAN'S WOUNDS were still pumping blood, which meant the killer was very close.

"Son of a bitch," Peary muttered.

"I'm thinking that's not the work of our boy," Jenkins said.

"How the hell would you know?" Peary growled.

"Because the gun he took when he ran from the kitchen didn't have a sound suppressor," Jenkins answered. "We would have heard this hit."

Peary realized Jenkins was right and didn't like what that meant. "So, we've got company."

"Cabriano or some of his goons?" Markinson wanted to know.

"Or the spooks maybe."

"Then I'm thinking," Jenkins said, "neither one of them wants to pay us off—unless it's like Grevey."

"Spread out. And don't panic," Peary said, moving away from the body, fearing it like there was some deadly virus he could catch.

Whoever Grevey's killer was, Peary knew it was all going to hell. But if they—whichever side—wanted them all dead why stop with Grevey? Was it a message? Telling them the price for failure was execution? Then why the games? Why not just charge out of the woods, or cut them down from the dark? Which side? How many? Dammit, none of it seemed right, they wouldn't be in this mess if Grevey had been on his toes.

Stow it. It was time to save the game, and his life.

Peary sensed they weren't alone, certain invisible eyes were watching. He cursed Grevey for letting Marelli get away in the first place. The SOB got what he deserved.

He thought he heard movement from behind, his heart lurching as he pictured what he'd just left, the Mossberg heavy and slippery in sweaty palms. He was spinning for his six when the silence was split by the chatter of autofire.

Peary heard shouting and glimpsed Markinson and Jenkins firing their weapons. One after the other they toppled in the periphery of green shimmer, weapons flying, arms flapping. He triggered the riot gun, bolting to his side, the thunderous retort piercing his ears. A warning cry in his head then told him he'd missed cutting down their attacker. In the next heartbeat Peary was certain of it, as he felt hot bullets tear through his flesh.

"WHERE THE HELL are you going? What kinda trouble you got yourself in now, Petey, huh? Hey, goddammit! You listening to me? This is still my place, I don't care if you paid for it or not! Bust in here, wake me up out of a dead sleep after your little hit-and-run, which wasn't all that great, case you were wonderin', but that's pretty much been your speed and style lately. And I don't appreciate you bringin' your goombahs in my home either, packin' heat for God and the whole world to see, neighbors spreading gossip, the big Mob boss's little whore on the side, look at her, what a fool is she! Plus your goombahs are stinkin' up my home with their booze and cigar fumes! Hey! I'm talking to you, big shot!"

Already flying across the living room, Cabriano gnashed his teeth as he shouldered past her, barreled into the bedroom and beelined for the closet, through explaining himself. He didn't have time for her crap, but she flew up his back, as he knew she would, a whirlwind of contention and cursing. He thought about his .45, pictured a quick delve inside his coat...

No.

Not with all the trouble falling on his head, disaster stalking him all over Brooklyn and beyond. One guy, it looked, was kicking his ass and taking names and his—and the cartel's—money. Cabriano let the volcano just rumble in his gut. For once he needed to be smart instead of impulsive. Frankie The Tube had confirmed the hit at the lot, but Cabriano could live with the loss of two more soldiers. What the hell was going on anyway? Who was behind wreaking all this havoc? Colombians? Spooks? The Feds? It was insane, all this trouble and terror, and when he was about to turn the corner, expand the empire, conquer the frigging world. Why now? Goddammit, why at all? Trust no one, damn straight. He was going hunting for answers, and heads.

The running was over.

Attempting to drown out her shrill voice, he seethed

over the image of the Fireball up in flames, a vision of his own world going up in smoke. An army of cops and firemen were right there at the bonfire, dirty rotten rat SOBs standing around, like they were ready to break out the hot dogs and marshmallows. From a safe distance he recalled how he watched them sipping coffee, smoking, a couple of them chuckling at the sight of his club burning to the ground. There were a few assholes in shields back there who were always in the Fireball, hitting on the girls, cheap scumbags who wanted to hang out all night, on his tab, like they were owed something to keep deaf, dumb and blind. Cabriano had been tempted to storm into their ranks and rail until kingdom come, but common sense took its grip. He needed to bail the city. The last thing he wanted was cops detaining him, his lawyers crying for days on end about billable hours, just to free him on bail from any list of charges, contrived or not. Right then, a slew of dire scenarios—growing by the minute—demanded a hands-on approach. He'd start in the Catskills, since if he wanted something done it looked like he had to do it himself.

He was opening the safe when Pauline cranked the screeching up another notch.

"What the fuck are you doin'! You takin' my money, I swear to…"

Enough.

Quickly he stuffed the small nylon bag with two hundred grand. There was more cash at his house, but, as bad as this nonsense was, he'd never escape the clutches of his own wife, not without firing a shot in anger. If, by chance, he needed more grease or walking around money he could call the casino, but that was assuming the Feds hadn't already shut it down.

He stood, turned and stared into the eye of the storm. She had to have read the look, sensed the cold deadly vibes. Pauline fell as quiet and still as he could ever recall.

"Do...not...say...another word."

She didn't, until Cabriano brushed past her.

He was in the living room, heading for his lieutenants, both men quickly looking away, as if they wished they could disappear through the floor.

"Don't come back!"

Cabriano had a response ready on the tip of his tongue, but his problems were far graver than any irate hit-and-run mistress. A few moments later, he discovered still more grief waiting in the alley beside her— his—brownstone. He looked past Frankie's crew of six, his heart skipping a beat at the sight of the three Towncars rolling his way. Cursing, he told his men to stand at ease, spotting a few hands inching for shouldered hardware.

The Towncars braked, single file, then doors opened to disgorge the Colombians.

Cabriano looked at the small, swarthy figure, watching, heart pounding, as José Hildago slipped between his gunmen.

"What's this?" Cabriano rasped. "You followin' me?"

Hildago bared a grin the Don pictured more on a hyena than anything human. "It would appear you are having some problems tonight, Señor Cabriano."

"It's under control."

"Is it now?"

"Listen, you and me, we'll talk later. I've got someplace to be—"

"Not so fast."

Cabriano broke stride, enraged as he found the Colombians spreading out, ready to go for broke as several of them draped the tails of leather trench coats over the butts of large handguns holstered on their hips.

Cabriano felt the bite of his own raw nerves as he laughed. "What the— I don't see this macho shit doin' much good for our future together, José. I got enough problems already."

"Yes. I know something of the nature of your problems." The smile broadened, Hildago spreading his arms. "That is why I am here to help."

ONLY THE BIG CATS were blessed with natural night vision. There were, however, the other senses, the nose and ears capable of picking up the slack when sight was almost nonexistent. There was also instinct and cunning, then a sensory web, his own honed, of course, from vast lethal experience of stalking human prey in the dark, in the densest forests and jungles on the planet. The enemy, he quickly discovered, shared none of these traits and skills, and it ended up killing them. In fact, their noisy bungle through the forest, combined with the smell of fear, the taint of panic in the air, and finally the worst of all unpardonable transgressions—running their mouths—led Bolan right to them. Call it instinct, common sense, good prior recon, a little help from the gods of war or a combo of all, but the Executioner found Marelli and the traitor four as if they shone beacons in the dawn. The shuffling sack of human misery that had been Grevey was the first to go. After that, the soldier could have nailed it down, but a whiff of Marelli's aftershave downwind put the task off until The Butcher was cuffed and quietly told the facts of life.

The Executioner walked up on Peary, M-16 aimed at the ASAC's spine as he crabbed for the combat shotgun, grunting and cursing. Bolan spit a fleck of bark off his lip where the traitor had blown off a hunk of tree with the Mossberg, inches from his face, throwing off the M-16's aim enough to spare the traitor a quick end.

Peary craned his head around, hesitated. "You? Son of a— Listen to me, Cooper. We get Marelli, there's money in it for you, lots of money. You can take half the cut from the others."

"I already have Marelli. What I need from you are answers."

Peary turned defiant. "Or what?"

"You're dead."

Whatever hope the man clung to faded as Bolan read the savage coming to life in his eyes. Peary was poised to scramble the final yard to the shotgun.

There was a time, not long ago, when Bolan wouldn't kill a lawman, no matter how dirty. But times changed, and the world, it seemed in certain quarters, had become a meaner, nastier, greedier, more vindictive place. Evil could just as easily walk behind a badge as it could hide anywhere else until it revealed itself. In fact, Bolan held those who were supposed to serve and protect—to defend the law against the lawless—more accountable.

Peary cursed and lunged. Bolan had no choice but to react. Then the man went still, eyes staring into forever. Quickly Bolan took Peary's radio and cell phone. He figured at least a few answers waited forty paces or so down the footpath.

Suddenly the Executioner heard the sound of chopper blades, coming from the north and closing fast. The soldier assumed the slaughter had been discovered again.

He slipped into deeper cover, opting to use the forest canopy for concealment instead of backtracking on the footpath. The question nagged Bolan: Was friend or foe on the way?

6

"I'm afraid I have some disturbing news."

John Rollins, assistant director of the Justice Department's Special Task Force on Organized Crime, grimaced. It was the third time he'd spoken to the electronically altered voice on the other end of his secured cell phone. He hoped it was the last he had to listen to the deep bass voice that sounded more robotic than human. Only he feared the future would soon find a face put to the ghost on the other end. It suddenly occurred to him, as he felt his guts knotting up, that perhaps he had already met the ghost during a clandestine midnight meet. Briefly, he recalled, when summoned over the phone to rendezvous with the cutout, he'd never seen more than a shadow in the night. Could it be that he was...did it matter?

"I already know what happened," Rollins snapped. "You didn't finish the damn job."

Rollins was pacing the living room of his Fairfax, Virginia, home. Up all night, tortured by images of all manner of perilous traps set in the path he was trodding, he'd been waiting for the ghost to report, but heard the news first from the director. Whatever phantom fears haunted him during the night, he knew they were howling to life with the new day.

"How in God's name…"

He looked around the empty room, the air locked in his chest, fear and rising panic bringing on the imaginings of ghosts of yesteryear. Not long ago, the big split-level house had felt like a cold giant cave when his wife walked out the door and divorced him. These days, he was grateful for any stretch of solitude he could steal. At present he wished he could hide under his roof until the storm blew past, specters from his own personal hell haunting him or not.

"Regrettable how it worked out, but it was unavoidable," Rollins heard the ghost tell him, as he marched into the kitchen, poured his fifth cup of coffee, considered then rejected the idea of spiking it with whiskey. He was overdue for a meeting with the task force director at the Justice Department. The morning news reported a major tie-up, a tractor trailer jackknifed on the interstate. As good an excuse as any, he figured, for keeping the director waiting on his arrival.

"What the hell happened out there?"

"We hit him three, maybe four times. What can I say? Man proved himself a tiger. County's finest showed up out of nowhere. I was forced to extract myself, lest I was forced into some unpleasantness with the police. You must also know I lost a good operator during the exchange. One, unlike some others, who is irreplaceable."

If that was an implied threat, Rollins chose to ignore it. "Yet another problem, you leaving his body behind."

"My friend, you are apparently just this side of clueless where our tactics and methods are concerned. The police will find no ID. Fingerprints and such will lead them into limbo, simply compounding the mystery. They can dial up the Almighty if they want, but it will be like my man never existed."

"You blew it, that's all I know. Do you know what this—"

"Silence! Find your balls and listen to me. This is a bed you helped to make, and you will sleep with the whore you chose."

Rollins scowled, wanted to read the riot act to the insolent SOB, but knew to some frightening extent his fate belonged in phantom hands.

"The operation on our end will proceed as scheduled, but there have been certain readjustments. Your infamous hit man witness, for one, has forced us to fine-tune certain measures that were already in place."

"What the hell are you talking about?" Rollins asked, hoping he'd masked his rising panic.

"You don't know?"

"Know what?"

The ghost chuckled. "Marelli has flown."

Rollins felt his knees buckle, his hand trembling, coffee sloshing onto the counter. Strangely enough, he was more angry than surprised. When Peary was late checking in by more than three hours, then wouldn't answer his calls, Rollins had feared the worst.

"Now what?"

"Fear not, ye of little faith," the ghost told him. "Steps have been taken. Two of our teams are in the area as we speak. One on the ground, one in the air. It's quite the mess, but everything is still salvageable."

"What steps?"

"You'll bear with me if I sound as if I'm attempting to impress you, which I have no need to do. But our power knows no bounds, no limits. Truth be told, we are a government within the government, perhaps we are the real government, carte blanche, licensed to… Well, you get the picture."

"I hear you talking a big game, but you're not saying a damn thing to put my mind at ease."

"If it's comfort and ease you desire…"

"Goddammit, I want to hear how you intend to handle this situation, not tell me how big your balls are!" Rollins shouted.

A long pause, then the ghost said, "A description of Cooper has already been passed on to all local and state law-enforcement agencies. This includes the FBI and Justice. The murders of four men from the Justice Department will be put on Cooper's head. If by some miracle he makes it out of New York, suspicion of what happened in Arlington earlier will likewise point his way."

Rollins shook his head, wondering how they—no, he—would pull off the whole insane juggling act. Cooper couldn't have been in two places at once, committing murder in two states hundreds of miles apart.

After the short sitrep from the director, though, Rollins understood why the ghost had wanted a copy of Cooper's file, complete with photo. Months back, when the plan was being engineered, bits and pieces of the bigger picture floated his way, and Rollins had been told to mail Cooper's jacket to a post-office box in Reno, Nevada. Whoever the spook, Rollins knew he had access to cutting edge technology. Apparently Cooper's Justice Department credentials had been found at the crime scene in Arlington, doctored by the ghost to pass as authentic. Where it all went next...

"Are you there?"

"Now what?"

"You go to work. Help run the investigation, the hunt for Cooper. Heat will come your way, but you've proved yourself capable of covering your tracks. I'm sure you remember Thailand?"

Rollins felt his stomach turn over, the memory of what led him to stare into the abyss of the present flamed to mind. He shut his eyes, cursing his life.

Several years back he'd been a field agent for the then-fledgling special task force. The department had been looking for a way to infiltrate the network of crime cartels in Southeast Asia. Rollins had worked hard to get the overseas assignment, seeking to advance his career, but also in search of adventure, sick and tired of monotonous routine. The fear he was going nowhere fast in both professional and personal life had become an obsession. He cajoled, he pleaded, he kissed the right asses to get the dream assignment. Oh, he'd found that something new and different, all right, and there was much dark truth to the cliche of a man being careful what he wished for. Looking back, it was his own beginning of the end, only he had no intention of getting consumed in the firestorm already burning out of control.

On the surface, the overseas operation back then had merit, he thought, a noble banner to fight the evils of the world he had raised himself. But he discovered his own terrible weaknesses along the way: drugs, white slavery, a thriving sex industry. Then there was murder for hire, bribery, corruption. Thailand was teeming with every conceivable vice. Eventually he had gone undercover, working loosely in tandem with men from other American intelligence agencies, his first encounter with the duplicitous ways of spookdom. The pit, he recalled, grimacing at the memory, had opened the night he murdered that prostitute, no more than a teenager, strangled with his bare hands when she wouldn't do what...

Enter the spooks with open arms and reassuring words, working their sorcery, brandishing his crime caught on film. Not to worry about the Bangkok police, his sins would never see the light, the spooks said. They had big plans for his future.

Talk about a pact with Satan.

Rollins heard himself make a choking noise.

"Hey, get your head back in the game."

Rollins jerked as the cold robot voice barked in his ear.

"That's what this is to you, isn't it? A game?" Rollins asked.

"Where the stakes could be the future of the human race, my friend. You need to start thinking about more than your own little world. Hear me good. You are a critical component in this, but you are a bit player, you are expendable. Your family has abandoned you, but it's funny how that worked out. Seeing as you abandoned them to chase your career. We are your only family left, probably always were."

"You rotten bastard."

"Remember that. Try and stick it to us, it would be better and quicker for you if you held a cobra in your hand. And remember—we'll be watching and listening. Carry on."

The ghost was gone.

Rollins felt the room spin, fighting down the sickness in his belly. He wanted to weep, run, hide.

But he knew he was stuck, locked in. And the prospect of life in prison or a sudden bloody demise at the hands of killers who could strike him down anywhere, anytime…

Rollins reached up and opened the cabinet, deciding he needed that drink, after all.

NO SOONER HAD HE TOLD Barbara Price about his failure to track down Brognola, than she hit him with the news. Though they lived in a world where violent death at the hands of the enemy could strike any time, Bolan felt as if he'd been run over by a train.

He'd pulled the Crown Victoria off the dirty track, concealing the commandeered vehicle behind thickets. Marelli was in the shotgun seat, the hit man staring through the jagged hole in the windshield, lost in what appeared to be gloomy thought, the picture-perfect wretch. To keep the professional killer's ears from burning and to avoid being sighted by their trackers in the Bell JetRanger, Bolan had settled between two dense rows of brush. Using the late Peary's cell phone, a series of cutout numbers were punched in until he was back channeled to Price's phone in her office at the Farm. He now split hard vigilance between the hit man and the surrounding woods, one hand grasping the M-16.

The Executioner listened with an angry and worried heart as the Farm's mission controller filled him in.

"He's in surgery, as we speak. I'm getting second-hand information from one of Hal's assistants. He's telling me it's bad, Mack. The left lung was punctured by one bullet, he took two other rounds through the ribs, but apparently they missed vital organs. My contact doesn't know much more at the moment, but from what he can gather, assuming massive blood loss to name just one problem, factor in his age, built-up stress from what we both know is a job that would take its toll on a man half his years...you've got the picture."

"It's fifty-fifty."

"I'm afraid, if that. I wish to God I could be there with him."

"I understand, and so would he."

"Meaning we'd be useless, sitting around in the waiting room while his would-be assassin is in the wind."

"That, and he would want us to carry on with the mission."

There was a heavy pause, and Bolan sensed the lady was grappling with the enormity of the moment, as, he knew, was the rest of the team at Stony Man. "How did you find out?" he asked.

"The local morning news. It's on every station. Two men gunned down, one dead, one believed to work for the Justice Department. Assailant or assailants fled, no motive and so forth. Plus I knew about his meeting. We both assumed from our earlier conversation they were two shadow operatives from pick-your-intelligence-agency."

"I'm familiar with the type. You said two men gunned down."

"Unidentified victim. Looks like Hal dropped one of the shooters."

"And any investigation to identify or track down the missing shooter or shooters will go nowhere."

"I get the feeling you may know something about Hal's attackers on your end."

Bolan fell silent for several moments, scanning the woods. With sunup, shafts of light were knifing through the forest canopy to clear away the deeper shadows. Bolan kept one ear tuned to the singing of birds, knowing any human encroachment would send them into a frenzy of squawking and flapping wings. He could feel time running out, his combat senses perk-

ing up, warning him nameless enemies were in the
vicinity.

"I have a hunch who's behind the hit on Hal, but I'm
going to need you to go a few extra miles on this one,
Barb. We're in this alone from here on." Quickly Bolan
brought her up to speed, told her what he needed and
suggested a plan of attack on her end.

She fell silent when he was finished, the soldier
thinking she was pondering the solutions too long.
Bolan asked, "Well?"

"Consider it done, but there's something else you
need to know. Mack," she said, pausing again. Bolan
listened to the mission controller draw a breath. "It's become a federal investigation, what with Hal getting
gunned down. Both the FBI and Justice agents were on
the scene before I spoke with my contact at the department. I was told they found your Justice Department ID
at the crime scene."

CABRIANO FIGURED it was all of a two-hour drive from
the city into the Catskills where they were heading. To
him the land was just a bunch of trees, hills and peaks,
figure a few lakes somewhere in the wilderness. He'd
never been here, nowhere close, hardly interested in
hiking, snowmobiling, camping, the sort of leisure, he
thought, best left to folks whose worlds didn't reach any
further than job and home.

The peasants.

He was in the back seat, nose full and head swim-
ming with whatever the sweet cologne Hildago was

doused in. The cartel's boy in New York was looking pretty smug, laying out dribs and drabs of the plan. Which was little more than full-scale slaughter of whoever got in their way, followed by, he had to admit, a pretty imaginative workout on Marelli until he turned over the disk. Full of assurances, too, how he was nothing but concerned that his problem—now their problem—was resolved. That, and their futures were shored up with their new mutual friends from the Middle East.

Cabriano kept glancing at his diamond-studded Rolex watch. Frankie had the lead vehicle, Cabriano's ride three down in the rolling Towncar convoy, with the lone beige Cadillac the odd wheels out. He was about to call The Tube, who knew the way from a prior payoff to their Justice guy—and why the hell was Peary not answering his calls?—when his cell phone trilled.

"Yeah?"

"Whatever it is you and your Colombian friends are planning, I suggest you abort, turn around and go back to the city."

"Who is this?" Cabriano snarled, fighting to keep the anxious edge out of his voice as he glanced at the dark look hardening Hildago's expression.

"A very interested third party."

Cabriano saw the big dark bastard boil up in his mind, all fire and thunder, like some avenging angel of death. But, steeling his composure, he knew the voice didn't belong to the nameless one-man wrecking crew who caused him so much grief, cost him a small fortune in money, not to mention lopping off his standing crew by about one-third.

"Whoever you are, I'm in no mood—"

"Stick your mood."

"Listen to me, you cock—"

"Look out your starboard window, three o'clock."

"Who is it?" Cabriano heard Hildago demand to know.

Waving off the Colombian, Cabriano was turning his head when the voice said, "Starboard would be to your right."

Cabriano scowling, searched for a reply that would save immediate face, but words eluded him.

Then he spotted the sleek chopper. It was sailing, low over hills swaddled in dense forest, holding a steady speed, four hundred yards or so out.

"Okay, so I see you, so…" Cabriano felt his blood boil. He was lord and master of an empire worth billions. Everywhere he went they bowed and scraped in his presence. Movie stars and sports heroes likewise couldn't kiss his ass enough. He could have anyone short of the President of the United States whacked, and the past twelve hours he'd been forced to swallow more turds, more shame, more disgrace…

Through the roar in his ears he made out the voice saying he could blow their little caravan off the road anytime he wanted, not enough pieces left to scrape into a dime bag. Didn't want to do that, left an *or else* hanging. Cabriano felt Hildago's nerves cracking. The guy was all over the seat, in his face. He threw a scowl at the Colombian and listened as he was told their special shipment was right then on the way to Colombia. They were expected in Colombia, no more than twenty-four hours from that moment. Woe be unto them should they not be there, and with the balance of the money for the special merchandise. The Marelli problem was in the process of being handled, but if he chose to proceed the price on several fronts would be taken to a new level that would leave him wishing prison was all he was facing.

Silence.

Cabriano ignored Hildago bleating in his ear, watched as the chopper veered off, fading into distant blue sky before it angled north, gathered speed, then punched through a layer of clouds.

"Answer me! Who was that?"

Cabriano looked at Hildago and told him, "Our spook friends have a message for us."

"ONE OF TWO THINGS is going to happen here, Marelli. Number one—you are going to take me to the disk. Do that, and as much as I'd just as soon shoot you and dump you by the road, I will see to it personally that you get your sweetheart deal. New program, new location, new agents picked and cleared by me."

They were heading what Marelli guessed was south, back to the city, the sun having almost cleared forested hills to the east. Nothing much by way of traffic, other than an SUV or recreation vehicle passing in the other lane every few minutes or so. But he kept thinking—

fearing—any second a battalion of angry or dirty cops would come swarming over them. A mile or so down the road, wind blowing through the gaping hole in the windshield, and flying glass slivers were no longer a threat. The big man didn't volunteer any information about how the hole got punched, and Marelli had weighty concerns other than the wind in his face. There was a jagged crack, angling up the windshield like a bolt of lightning, but it didn't obscure the man's vision.

Marelli stared at the stranger. Gut and experience told him the man had traveled some dark roads in his day. Marelli knew a killer when he saw one—it was in the eye, the voice, the way a guy carried himself. Like he'd walked through fire before, no big deal, bring it on, seen worse. Whoever he was, really worked for— Fed, spook, one of those black ops of the military— there was something genuine about the man he couldn't quite put a finger on. An honesty perhaps, something inside the heart he believed in, would go the distance to defend. What the hell was this? he wondered. Was he finding himself trusting, liking the man?

Marelli punched in the dashboard lighter. "You're tellin' me those weren't your boys who ate up their own back there, wanted to string me up by my nuts."

"That's what I'm telling you."

Marelli bobbed his head. The cuffs were tight, but his hands weren't bound hard enough to cut off blood and swell them to purple balloons. Even if he thought he could wriggle free, he knew the man was, indeed, either his salvation or doom.

"Clock's running, Marelli."

The mobster lit his smoke, eased back in the seat. "Guess I don't have to ask what number two thing is if I don't cooperate."

"You're a smart guy."

Marelli grunted. "Yeah. For someone with a fourth-grade education. Okay." He nodded, blew smoke and said, "It's in Miami. My girl's sittin' on it. Now, I need this new program of yours in writing."

"You can carve my word in stone."

For some reason, Marelli believed that. He smoked, thinking some angry change had taken hold of the man after his phone call back in the woods. Whatever it was—bad news most likely—he sensed the killer inside the guy more ready and determined than ever to take this ride to the end.

Marelli looked at the man. "Mind if I turn on the radio?"

"Go crazy, but not too loud."

Marelli turned on the radio, began twisting the dial, knowing there was a soft rock or country station some-where in these hills. "Mind if I ask where we're goin', what's the plan?"

"You're going home."

"Miami?"

"There first. And the plan's to keep both of us breathing."

The man suddenly snapped off the radio, and Marelli was startled by the sudden silence. Then he saw the fleet rolling around the bend in the road. Marelli glanced back and forth from the big guy to the black-tinted windows on the Towncars and Cadillac, the man not showing the first sign of nerves. As the last car blew by, Marelli said, "You know who that is?"

"I know exactly who it is," the man said.

Marelli rolled down the window, cleared the smoke. He looked over his shoulder and saw a string of brake lights.

7

Simple but grim either way, Bolan knew the options were flight or fight. Both had merit, and risks that could slam the brakes on the whole campaign any stretch of the road. Given the stakes—a purported superradioactive toxin used for rocket fuel, meant to propel astronauts into deep space at light speed on alleged nuclear propulsion, and now for sale to fanatics in search of the leviathan of all dirty bombs—and circumstances—his own head on a platter for impalement at the hands of the good guys—the latter outweighed the former. But there were other considerations—such as noncombatants and good cops who didn't know any better—that made running more practical for reaching the next goal. And getting his hands on Marelli's disk, not to mention keeping both of them alive, was the only priority at that moment of the new day.

They still had a way to go—ninety minutes or so, depending on traffic—before making the Big Apple's outer limits, and some road warrior-style rampage on a well-traveled highway, sure to maim or kill innocent motorists, was last on the soldier's list for a call to arms. Pull into a campground, diner, gas station, thinking the vicious jackals might rein in lethal intent on account of witnesses? No, Bolan didn't find that wise either, not if he factored in desperate men of violence who would go to any extreme to save their world. Collateral damage to them was just the peripheral cost of keeping the empire flourishing. Keep going, then, turn the Crown Vic into a NASCAR torpedo to the end of the coming finish line? Hope the gods of war would carry him on the wings of divine guidance until he barreled across the tarmac, aimed like a bullet for the hangar at Newark International? There again, a rocket ride all the way to the city limits carried yet more dim prospects of a clean finish, since the last sight he wanted looming on his tail was strobing lights.

Trouble, real or phantom, was plaguing Bolan's thoughts, the more he pondered the dilemma. Flight or fight, damned if he didn't.

He was no stranger to New York and New Jersey, and if he chose to keep the breakneck pace, the soldier knew the quickest route to Newark International. But there was no telling—despite Barbara Price stepping in with capable hands and clout that reached the White House—what would be on tap when he attempted to board the Gulfstream, Miami bound, with the songbird of the ages, and who was on the gallows for at least three, maybe four tribes of hostiles to hang. One seemingly insurmountable Mount Everest hurdle at present was that he could be certain the conspiracy inside the Justice Department wound its tentacles up the hierarchy, or no way could Peary have pulled off quadruple murder and skip off after Marelli with no worries about a full-scale investigation.

As far as the tightening noose around his own neck went, Price was already thrusting an iron in that particular fire. Trouble was, a dark cloud of suspicion he may have gunned down Hal Brognola was hung on his head. Which meant dragnets, roadblocks, APBs, BOLOs, good cops walking blindly into the whole sordid murk where the big sharks passed off the chum— SAC Matt Cooper—in hunt of the main course.

Bolan gathered speed, pedal to the metal, shooting them down open highway with the speedometer's needle holding at 90 mph. In the corner of his eye, the soldier spotted Marelli giving his neck muscles a workout, the soldier feeling the hit man's nerves cracking as he twisted on the seat. Another hard look into the sideglass, and Bolan saw the four-Towncar-lone-Cadillac convoy swing around, tires blowing out smoky vapor in the distance as tread clawed asphalt. There was a mile gap from their pursuers, but the wheelman of the point Towncar didn't much care about the speed limit.

Then fate stepped in and made the decision for Bolan.

How he'd missed the state trooper, where he'd even barreled onto the highway from was a moot point. Marelli was muttering a curse, wanting to know the plan, and Bolan eased off the gas. Careening around a bend, fighting to keep from flying off the road for a long drop into a deep ravine, the warrior spotted yet two more sleek New York troopers shooting cruisers down in the southern distance. There, both cruisers rolled on but were slowing, lights flashing, as they next went into a long dramatic slide. That maneuver alone raised the red flag in Bolan's head that the word on Cooper was out. The two-cruiser barricade could be navigated, around or through, but Bolan knew the running stopped there.

Hemmed in front and back, two sides wanting his hide, good and bad guys, the soldier tapped the brakes, swinging onto the shoulder. Slowing, he searched the forested hills, something telling him the Bell JetRanger was in the area, and that the occupants were responsible for tagging his vehicle, sticking the law up his tailpipe. Lights and sirens bearing down on his rear, Bolan reached over the seat and hauled in both M-16/M-203 and the HK subgun.

"No matter what happens," Bolan told Marelli, "do not leave the car."

"Ain't the cops I'm worried about, pal. You think Cabriano and boys give a rat's ass about a few smokies gettin' in their way? Oh, yeah, I'll sit tight, unless you get yourself cut to ribbons and blown off the planet."

Bolan opened the door.

"ARE YOU INSANE, Cabriano? We can't just kill policemen, not out on a public highway, not unless we want the full wrath of—"

"Why not, José? You do it all the time in your country. Judges, lawyers, cops, you wipe out bloodlines of whole families what I hear. Silver or lead, isn't that what you people say in Colombia?"

"That is different! This is hardly the same situation."

"The hell it isn't. I'm passing the order on to my guys, so shit or get off the pot! But you decide to sit out the fight, I'll remember it, believe you me!"

Cabriano left the Colombian to flail and fume, punching in the numbers to Frankie's line. He took in the situation ahead. The Colombian goons up front were throwing evil eyes all around, Cabriano thinking that big shotgun in the hands of the wild-eyed hardman in the passenger seat was inching up his way. He spotted three smokies in all, with two cruisers down the highway, blocking any southbound escape, one sliding in behind the big nameless bastard who had somehow bagged Marelli. That alone stirred up another hornet's nest of maddening questions. What had happened to Peary and his shooters? Who was this one-man juggernaut? What did he want? What the hell was his game? For one thing, no Fed he'd ever heard of was granted the full blessing of the law to run amok, burn, blast and slaughter at will. Last time he looked this wasn't a Third World hellhole run by some dictator who could march out kill squads at whim to wipe out malcontents, rebels and such. Then there were constitutional rights, whether a man was accused of crimes or not. He was owed his day in court, whatever the government thought they had on him. They couldn't cut loose their own hired gun on him and his people, if that's what happened back in Brooklyn.

It occurred then to Cabriano the troopers could have radioed for backup, meaning the dread possibility of roadblocks all the way to New York. But Cabriano saw the future going up in flames if he didn't act out in wild desperation to hold up the crumbling walls. If they lost here, the future didn't matter.

The Tube growled on the line. Cabriano told him what to do, and if he had any problems following those orders...

"Understood, boss. I'll pass it on."

But Cabriano wasn't so sure he understood at all. Frankie sounded gun-shy to him.

"Get your driver to hang back, José, in fact, pull off to the side of the road," Cabriano snarled as the narco-middleman bared teeth, shaking his head. "There's no time to dick around here! In or out? I'll go it alone, me and my guys, I have to. You understand it's your ass and the asses of the whole goddamn Quintero Cartel if I don't get that disk? Know this, too. That big bastard you seen sitting on Marelli? He's responsible for either blasting up or taking about twenty million hard-earned dollars that were supposed to go to your people!" That, Cabriano found, grabbed Hildago's undivided attention.

"Why, may I ask, are you just telling me this now, when we have been riding together for more than two hours?" Hildago looked dangerously angry.

"Because I've been looking for a way to save the whole game before we lose everything, that's why."

Hildago laughed. "Really?"

The first words out of Hildago's mouth to his wheelman were in Spanish. Cabriano barked, "English, god-dammit! I wanna know if you're on board or gonna stab me in the back!"

"DROP THE WEAPONS!"

Bolan was unfolding, halfway out the door, M-16 leading his rise, when he knew it was beyond hope.

"Do it! Now!"

The soldier held out the Justice Department creden-tials for the trooper to inspect, though he was grimly aware he had to have appeared to be exactly what the man suspected he was. It was crystal clear to Bolan in the lawman's tone and stance he was a moment away from opening up with his Glock.

"I'm Cooper, Justice Department," Bolan shouted back, as the Towncar blew by the trooper. The soldier felt his gut coiling, four sets of potential doom tearing his vigilance, front and rear.

"I know who you are!" the trooper roared, but his own angry stand, partly shielded as he was in the gap of his door, became distracted, eyes darting from the Towncar on the fly past his roost to the vehicles jerk-ing to a stop on his rear.

"Those men behind you are coming to kill me and my federal witness! Forget what you might think you know about me, get in your car and get the hell out of here!"

The trooper was half turned to Bolan when four hardmen burst out the door of the Towncar on his bumper. A mixed bag of shotguns, pistols and subma-chine guns filling their hands, they opened fire on the lawman without warning.

FRANKIE TRIED to focus his thoughts on the insane order he was about to carry out. Other than the odd 12-gauge pump shotgun in the hands of Vinnie Caputo behind him, Ingram MAC-10s were the cop killer of choice. He wished he was anywhere right then but roaring down a public highway toward two state troopers who were already waving pistols at them, hollering, it looked, to get out of the way, pull over. The notion that Cabriano had sent them on to waste two state troopers put something as close to the fear of God in him as he'd probably known in the six years he'd been a top lieutenant in the Family. It was one thing to shake down local bookies and dealers, beating them with fists or tire irons until they were a blubbering crimson worm willing to pay all kinds of tribute to the Family. One thing, also, to gun down rival wise guys, or even on occasion forced to execute a Family member who either stole from the till or was turning rat, like The Butcher.

But killing cops? They gave the needle to cop killers in New York, and he had a wife and four kids to think about. The other wise guys could play the mistress shenanigans, hang out at the Fireball all night if they wanted, but he stayed with Cabriano out of necessity—to pay the bills and put food on the table, not to indulge a playboy lifestyle, risk hearth and home, carousing, every day a party. Hell, he even kind of liked his wife. Not like the other wise guys, always bellyaching about this and that, never happy, no matter what, the grass always greener in some other broad's bed.

Lately he'd been thinking he wanted out. Just walk away before it was too late, he was too old, or in prison or dead. But with a grade-ten education, where else was he going to make the kind of money Cabriano doled out? No, he couldn't quite see himself flipping burgers, pushing a mop, playing squeegee bum in rush-hour traffic....

Stuck, then. At least for now.

A glance at their wheelman, a look over his shoulder at the others, and he could tell by the grim set to their features they were more than up for wasting cops. Like this would be some badge of honor. He could hear the bragging already when they were clubbing, getting loaded, embellishing their own roles, no doubt. Hell, he wouldn't put it past any of them to take the shields, guns, hats, some trophy from the kill, for impressing the broads and other wise guys. Which, together with them running their mouths, was sure to bring heat.

Man, when this was over, when they were back in New York, he was going to grant Babs her wish, quit this gangster nonsense. Go find a real honest job. Be a man instead of a bum. His heart wasn't in it anymore. At the moment, he couldn't agree more with her, thinking of the shame, how much she would loathe what he was about to become if she could see him now. What would she, the kids, do, him spending his last few years on death row?

He felt the Towncar lurching to a halt, the image of Babs in tirade vanishing. With tinted windows, the troopers couldn't see in, he knew, but something had to have raised the alarm in their heads as one of them broke from his barricade, marching out into the open, barking at them to get out of the car.

Frankie hung back a moment, aware he had no choice but to follow through. The others were bursting out their doors, going for it. The thunderous explosion of their weapons jolted him into the terrible reality of no return, his hand shuddering out to open the door. The troopers were returning fire, glass spiderwebbing before his eyes as it took a round or two. Frankie glimpsed the big holes spurting blood across the troopers' chests and figured they were already dead on their feet. He decided he had to at least make a show of it, heaving his three-hundred-plus pounds into the murderous fray, Ingram up, tracking the trooper already absorbing hits behind his cruiser. He was holding back on the trigger, the first few rounds stuttering loose, when the chopper seemed to drop in out of nowhere. Frankie thought he heard Ralino or one of the others shouting, their weapons roaring on, but it was impossible to home in on any sound other than the piercing whine of rotor blades, the squall of rotor wash. Frankie squinted against the wind, firing on both troopers now toppling. The chopper swung around, hovering behind the cruisers. Frankie looked up, glimpsed the white metal skin sparking a second or two, aware Ralino and the others were tattooing the whirlybird, insane with bloodlust. Frankie stole a heartbeat's view of a figure in a black helmet, visor hiding his face, hunched behind what looked to him like some kind of cannon. He counted five, maybe six barrels, wondered briefly who the new arrival was and did it matter, when the cylinder began spinning, smoking and blasting.

Frankie knew the others were taking hits, their screams whipped away by the roaring monster above. He was bringing his Ingram on target, his face slashed by flying glass, metal shards and hot blood, when the doomsday gun swung his way.

BOLAN KNEW THERE WAS nothing he could do but save himself and Marelli while savaging the enemy. Figure the opposition was desperate enough to the point of insanity, gunning down lawmen in broad daylight on a public road, telling Bolan they would go to any extremes to capture or slay Marelli. The addition of the chopper, clearly custom-built to turn it into a gunship, was a lethal problem the soldier knew he'd have to deal with in short order. There was nothing he could do for any of the troopers. Cabriano's goons mowed down the lawmen without hesitation. But payback for the cold-blooded murder was instant. The Gatlin gun ripped through the mobsters' ranks in two shakes. That beast of firepower was capable of pounding out thousands of rounds, devouring flesh in great chunks of exploding gore. The Towncar was all but lost, sheared apart in the barrage. Discount that helmeted shooter on the Gatling as Justice or FBI, and Bolan had to believe more spooks from some No Name Agency were on-hand to heap more misery into someone's life.

Bolan had serious problems of his own to contend with.

Judging from the swarthy faces and fancy threads of the four shooters who took out the lone trooper, then catching a word or two of snarled Spanish, Bolan had to figure them for cartel thugs. Come to help Cabriano with his Marelli situation, collect money, hammer out their deal. He intended to send them on their way to hell like the crime boss and the spooks.

The trooper was down, nerve spasms capping off two rounds from his pistol, when the Executioner tapped the M-203's trigger. Coasting past the cruiser, the warhead detonated on the grille of the lead Town-car. The blast proving a great equalizer, the fireball kicked four mauled screamers in all directions.

Eight down. Reckon four to a vehicle, and the odds were close to cut in half.

Marching ahead, dumping another 40 mm frag bomb down the launcher's gullet, the soldier veered into the space between his Crown Vic and the cruiser. Wreckage banked the Cadillac next in line, howling gunmen bobbing and weaving. Their dance steps through the flotsam gave Bolan all the edge he needed to begin dispensing autofire. They were flailing under his M-16 bombardment, wild shotgun blasts and sub-gun fire peppering the Caddie, when Bolan felt the gunship blowing rotor wash up his back.

The Executioner hit the deck as the air was lanced by the heavy metal thunder of the Gatling gun.

8

John Rollins feared the future, saw the shortening to-
morrows like a comet flaming out, crashing to Earth,
pictured himself squashed beneath the rock. At the moment, he couldn't decide if he felt more intimidated by
the portraits of the attorney general and President of the
United States hung on the wall behind the director's
desk, or the former Marine gunnery sergeant appearing
to him like a grim picture of fire and brimstone in the
burning flesh. All seemed to bore dagger eyes into his
soul, in search of hidden dark truths, the eyes glaring
without blinking as Rollins sat in the leather chair, waiting for the director to get off the phone. Whoever Worthy was speaking to only seemed to darken his mood.
The director's stare was feeling to Rollins as if the man
was on the edge of learning what would most certainly
lead to prison bars slamming shut on his backside.

Rollins heard, "And you are? And you come by this
information how? Or are you just guessing, maybe have
your own agenda, lady?"

Rollins didn't like the sound of that, not one damn
bit. The director's knuckles were popping as if he

wanted to crush the phone into dust in a fist he imagined could crush a grown man's entire skull and face.
There were stories about Worthy, tales from Gulf I, still
circulating in the halls of Justice. The younger bucks
practically bowed down and kissed the ground before
this crew-cut bulldog who paced more muscle than a
young Arnold. The Medal of Honor winner was a devout Catholic, a family man and no-nonsense by the
book.

Rollins felt his blood pressure rise, pulsing in his eardrums.

Two stiff belts before leaving for the office, and getting bogged down in traffic hadn't done much to calm
the storm inside Rollins. The initial crime scene reports in his lap perused, he had just learned from FBI
agents at the lodge that all eight men assigned to guard
Marelli were dead. Peary and his killing band had apparently been slain themselves in the woods, not far
from the lodge. There were also three unidentified victims strewed in the massacre at the lodge, apparently
having engaged in a firefight with suspect or suspects
undetermined, but blown to smithereens by ordnance
that was not part and parcel of Justice Department operations. The mystery compounded, but Rollins had a
good idea who was behind all the mayhem, which was
why he'd put out an APB on SAC Matt Cooper. Cutting the red tape to dump the man on the FBI's Most
Wanted list might prove a tough sell, but he'd been
pondering the problem all night, certain his litany of rationales would pan out. He would sway the director to

have Cooper hunted down like a wild animal. Then there was the gnawing fear—no, terror—that Brognola would pull through, point the blame in his direction. It would be easy enough to add two and two on that score, since he was responsible for marching the man into the ambush in the first place.

The day held nothing but the promise of unending dread and anxiety. Future? What future?

Worthy put down the phone. Rollins looked at the man, hoping he'd fill him in on what was clearly a disturbing call.

"Who was that?" Rollins asked, aware of the sudden outbreak of sweat on his forehead.

Instead of answering, Worthy, peering, sniffed the air. "Have you been drinking?"

Rollins fidgeted, silently cursing the man for pursuing what, in his mind, was a snare to make his day yet more miserable, or an excuse to send him packing off the investigation. He hoped to God he hid the simmering resentment in look and tone, as he told him, "I, uh, well, uh…yes, sir. Considering the gravity…well, what with the murders…"

"Spare me all that lame bullshit. I need everyone's head in the game, clean and sober. I need all my people sharp, hungry, alive. We're looking at the mother of AFUs, and I don't have the first goddamn clue, the first answer as to how, why, or who blew this shitstorm in our faces."

Before Rollins could jump-start his battery of theories, truths, half-truths and good old-fashioned bull-

shit, the former gunnery sergeant hauled open a desk
drawer, produce a fifth of Wild Turkey and slammed it
on his desktop.

"See that, Assistant Director Rollins?"

Did he ever. Half-empty, by his reckoning, he was
thinking the man would offer him a shot, an olive branch
before the real ass-reaming started, a softening of the
blow.

"Your point is noted, sir."

"I don't think so, Rollins. That's my personal stash,
the one indulgence I allow myself," he gruffed, then
fired up a cigar, taking his time, working up a nice fat
cloud to blow across the desk. "I do two, no more, no
less, each day, end of day, when the day's business is concluded. Then I go home to my wife and children. Spend
quality time with them, help with dinner, homework and
so forth. Make love to my wife three, sometimes four
times a week still after fifteen years of being married to
the same woman. Go to sleep for a few hours, get up well
before the sun, jog, pump some iron, bone up on the
day's agenda, get my ass to work. No matter how tough
the coming day, I go get it, shoulders squared, no hinky
alterations in routine. Whining and weakness are for
guys on the way out. That in mind, do I need to spell out
your tomorrow if I smell whiskey on your breath again?"

"No, sir. I understand."

The bottle disappeared, Rollins thinking the man
flashed him a dubious scowl.

"Now, you want to tell me where we are in this shitstorm?"

"All indications, sir, we are looking at a renegade agent."

"Cooper, again. Your supersecret agent black ops pal of Brognola."

"Yes, sir."

"Stop right there. I've read the man's jacket thoroughly, ever since you started pissing in my ear with your conspiracy theories. He's been part of Brognola's special task force for a number of years now, and the way I'm hearing it from up top there's some things better left unknown. Yeah, he's probably former military, intelligence, some things raise a few questions, granted. Likewise I can read between a few lines, gaps in his service record, after action reports on certain operations where the Justice Department, namely Brognola's office, swept double-digit body counts into a black hole."

"My whole point, sir. My fear is he's the renegade responsible for the attempt on Brognola's life and in all likelihood the massacre in the Catskills."

Worthy grunted. "How do you figure that? Unless he's a ghost I don't see him being in two places at once."

"My theory is a team of two or three operators, under Cooper's command, one in New York, one down here in our neck of the woods. Cooper jetting to and from, military flights from the looks of it, arranged, I think, through Brognola's office. Problem is, all this smoke and mirrors, I can't say at this time—"

"That's a fact. You aren't saying a goddamn thing, but I'm feeling smoke getting blown up my ass."

Rollins winced, felt his chest tightening. "Sir?"

"You don't show me the first inkling of proof, not a scintilla of fact."

"There's his ID…."

"A plant. A ruse, Rollins. You ever hear of misdirection?"

"Do you know something I don't, sir?"

Worthy eased back in his chair, peering through the cloud of cigar smoke. "I just got off the phone with a lady who claims she knows both Brognola and Cooper. Claims she's worked with them in the past. Mystery woman."

"Easy enough to run a trace on the—"

"Yeah, and find it all leading into so many cutouts I'd end up running off, screaming into the night."

"And she told you what, exactly?"

"Gist of it, tells me Cooper's clean as one of heaven's angels, above-board and beyond reproach."

"And you believed her?"

"I don't know, I really don't know at this point."

Rollins sensed Worthy holding back and opted for misdirection of his own. "How, uh, what's the status on Brognola, sir?"

"His status?" Worthy gruffed, paused, smoked, measured.

"What I meant—"

"He's out of surgery, in ICU, his life hanging by a thread. He took one through the lung. They plugged it up, but the doctor told me it was a miracle he made it to the emergency room at all, what with blood loss, all the blood swelling up the lung. The man near choking to death on blood alone."

Now Rollins did square those shoulders, put on that brave face Worthy just talked about. "That's great news, sir. I'm happy for the man. I understand his family is by his side. I'm sure they're greatly relieved." Rollins fell silent, the stare in the clouds sending an ice shiver down his spine.

"Right."

"You'll keep us posted?" Rollins asked.

"Right. Where were we? Oh, yeah. You want me to drop Cooper on the FBI's Most Wanted list. Seems, though, you already jumped the gun, nearly did that without this office's nod. Just got off the phone with our people in New York. Apparently you already lit a fire under the man, got him on the way to the hangman."

"Sir, I get the feeling you're not understanding my position, my concerns."

"Call me a big dumb-ass jarhead. Why don't you spell it out."

"We know virtually nothing about this Cooper, other than what Brognola wants everyone to know—and I'm thinking the man's jacket was created by Brognola in the first place. Classic smoke screen. We have a walking mystery, what looks a gunslinger with carte blanche, a proved track record that defies normal federal procedures and guidelines, the manual thrown out the window in what many would consider clear breaking of this country's laws. Why, if you look at all the bodies alone…"

"Rumor."

"Then the AA reports. Hear the talk from agents in the field who have worked with the man. Put it all together, the glaring assumption—"

"Hold it right there. I don't have to spell out what assume means, or do I?"

"Ass of u and me."

"In this case it could end careers. Look, Rollins. We both know what you call a special project—black op— is not all that unusual in our line of work. The public never hears about it, of course, but we know of extreme operations…"

"I wasn't aware the Justice Department had the authority to issue what amounts to a license to kill," Rollins said, taking a chance.

"They don't, and we don't know for a fact that they are."

"Sir, I'm assuming you know about the string of attacks on the Cabriano Family, and only hours ago? While our people were being slaughtered and Brognola was gunned down…"

"I do, in fact. And you're implying?"

"I smell the work of Cooper."

"Word I get from our people in New York, it's either gangland competition or the Don's Cali amigos. Then again, maybe it's these spooks with their purported batch of radioactive waste from outer space."

"My money's on Cooper."

"The man can damn near walk on water, to hear you tell it. Now he's in three places at once. A man like that, a miracle worker, he oughta be able to do damn well what he pleases."

Rollins bit down his rising anger and frustration. This was going nowhere fast. And Worthy, he sensed, was baiting him, but why?

"Tell you what, Rollins. You get me proof Cooper is this mad-dog gunslinger, I'm talking hard concrete no-shit evidence, and by the end of the day's business. Right now, I've got far more on my plate than spinning wild tales about a man who appears to have the hand of God on him."

"And you don't see a problem with that?" Rollins asked, feeling queasy.

"Listen to me. We have slain men who fell under the protective sanctity of various departments within this building, not to mention families they left behind who are going to want some answers and, if they don't get them to their satisfaction will be on every talk show— you want to talk conspiracy theories then? Then we have a federal witness on the run who could bring down the Cabriano operation, A to Z, who was going to give us the Quintero Cartel, Mideast terrorists and who claims to have set up the whole dirty damn deal with spook out west for this extraterrestrial material. In other words, we have damn serious work to do, questions to answer. You sitting there pissing and moaning about something you can't prove is a waste of our time. One more thing, then you're dismissed. My mystery lady? Before she hung up, she claimed to have proof that what happened to our people in New York was engineered from within our department."

Rollins felt his heart skip a beat. "Really? A voice on the phone, no name. You're not telling me you find her a credible source."

"I'm not going to be as quick as I sense you want to be to dismiss what she told me. One thing I have to consider—she had this number, which, as we both know, is a secure line."

Rollins put on what he hoped was the appropriate curious face, hoping there was no fear in his voice as he said, "I'll leave that end of it to you, sir. In the meantime, I have a lot of work to do."

"I want you to keep me abreast, every hour, on the hour. Understood?"

Gathering up his crime-scene report, Rollins stood on trembling legs, his heart thundering in his ears as he felt the full drilling impact of three sets of eyes. "Yes, sir."

"And Rollins?"

He turned, steadied himself somehow. "Sir?"

"If this turns out to be an inside job, if there are snakes under our roof, if this is about taking Mob money, may God have pity on them. Because I will not. And believe me, I will get the truth."

Rollins nodded that he understood, then headed for the door. If looks could kill, he thought, the eyes he felt watching him on the way out would have dropped him, in his tracks, a bullet to the back of his head. The director wanted proof, he thought, but evidence of whose guilt?

AD John Rollins felt his stomach churn. It was over, the only hanging question was, how far could he run?

ANOTHER TIME, ANOTHER battlefield, and Jimmy Marelli would have enjoyed the front-row seat, watching the big man work, laying odds he'd beat the Cabriano-Cali house. Funny right then how time froze up. Three killing grounds opening up at almost the same instant, his life on the line, no less. No telling how many SOBs in the whole dirty rat pack were there to snuff him, or cuff him for a slice-and-dice party until he gave up the disk. Despite the fear of the moment, he couldn't help but admire the warrior—realized all of a sudden he didn't even know the man's name. No sooner was the smokey dropping, than the big man pumped one grenade smack into the lead Towncar. The four-pack of jackals was blown away in the whirlwind of fire, smoke and flying metallic trash.

Road kill.

Which, he feared, was exactly what he would be, when he caught sight of the sleek warbird skimming the highway on the soar, then twisting. That big stainless-steel spinning cannon ripping the world apart, it seemed, in his face. He stole one final and what he knew was a foolish heartbeat to watch the big bastard mow down a few standing hardcases, then knew it was time to make his own move.

As the first tidal wave of bullets washed over the Crown Vic, Marelli bulled his shoulder into the door, the snarl of rage lost to the sudden din. The noise of rotor wash and the ear-splitting sound of that mammoth whirling machine gun drove the fear of the devil, from tingling scalp to aching feet. The drumming of heavy lead was like a locust swarm times ten thousand, he imagined. He was out the door, thrust, it felt, on living squall of sound and fury, falling just as he heard glass explode and metal groan under the barrage. He felt the swirling wrath of wind, the storm of glass, the merciless roar of weapon fire, his gut telling him he'd cleared the bombardment by a hair.

Marelli slammed down, air driven from his lungs. He buried his nose in the earth, held on and hoped for the best, but feared the worst. They were screaming somewhere close by, the eerie but thunderous drumming of those big slugs chewing up man and machine cleaving his senses.

Instinct told him the shooter in the belly of the flying beast had passed him by, assumed him waxed.

Fine by him.

Marelli began to crawl toward the slaughter. He needed to know the score. Depending on who was still standing after this mother of all bloodbaths...

Well, the only way to find out, he figured, was to keep crabbing on for the eye of the storm. For some reason, he found himself pulling for the big nameless one-man army. Some damn long odds, just the same, even for that guy, and if he was one of the casualties...

He'd figure out his next move, if that was the case. He was a survivor, after all. He'd seen plenty of killing and walked away before, middle finger to his slain dead, but he had to admit he'd never experienced this kind of slaughter.

The hell raging ahead, he thought, took The Butcher's work to a whole new level.

FOR ALL OF TWO SECONDS, Cabriano was certain they'd pull off the hit. That was before the warbird dropped onto Frankie and the boys and chopped them up, down and all around like sausage meat shoved through a grinder. Whatever the fearsome weapon blazing away in the hands of the helmeted figure, his personal problem as of last night compounded his terror.

When the lead Towncar was lost in a fireball and the black-clad shooter started scything down their combined forces, working his field of fire, stem to stern, the warning bell in Cabriano's brain gonged loud enough to split his brain with a fresh wave of horror.

"Call your driver back!" he shouted at Hildago. "Get us the fuck outta here! Now, goddammit!" he roared, as the warbird swooped down, closing the gap in seconds flat, angling around.

And the sky began falling on man and machine, so suddenly, swiftly and terribly, it struck Cabriano as if a divine lightning rod of retribution had come to punch all their tickets.

Paralyzed, Cabriano watched as the rolling wave of lead sheared roofs and hoods off the vehicles in front like flimsy tin cans, glass storms tearing through figures darting away from the hellish blitzkrieg, guys howling, grabbing at their faces and eyes, useless weapons hurled away. He felt his sphincter pucker, but losing control of bladder and bowels was the least of his terrors. Shame he might be able to live with, provided he was still breathing in the next few seconds.

Hildago, he heard, was screaming for Jorge or Ochoa or both—but Cabriano only needed one of them.

He got his wish. Their wheelman knowing no way in hell could he avoid the coming wrath, was practically flying through the door, tossing his subgun on the seat.

"Back up! Get us outta here!" Cabriano bellowed, aware next of Hildago matching him in both volume and tone of terror.

The world kept blowing up before Cabriano as the wheelman launched them in reverse.

Cabriano roared at the wheelman, as he shimmied all over the seat, nearly dumped in Hildago's lap.

Cabriano kept hollering as the wheelman and Hildago went back and forth in Spanish, arguing, he hoped about the quickest flight path the hell out of there. The terror bulging the wheelman's eyes telling him he didn't care which direction, as long as it was far from the flying man-eater.

Cabriano found himself kissing the door's upholstery, as the Towncar's back end whipped to the side without warning. He was ready to pull his weapon, shoot the wheelman, who kept babbling in Spanish, then commandeer the vehicle himself when he became aware of a faint trilling. The unholy racket of the gates of Hell diminished as it dawned on him the sound belonged to his cell phone. He grabbed the instrument, the thought fleeting in his mind that this was some sick joke being played on him by unforgiving fate.

A phone call? At a time like this?

He wanted to scream at Hildago's driver to stop shooting them in reverse down the narrow dirt trail—trees and brush and big rock blurring past—before they crashed and burned, but fear and curiosity found him punching on before he knew it.

"Yeah!"

"Why are you running?"

Cabriano caught the strain of his own laugh. He couldn't believe it, sure terror had carved off any last shred of sanity.

"What?"

"What are you so afraid of?"

"You gotta be shitting me!"

"I told you," he heard the ghost on the other end say, "I came to help. Truth be told, Peter, I'm here to rescue you."

He was about to tell the voice of all this big help where he could stick his version of saving the day when Hildago's scream pierced the air. The car slammed into some unyielding object and Cabriano lurched back, spine and neck contorting with the force of the collision. He felt his head hammer off the ceiling next, stars blasting in his eyes. Then he was grabbing at air, joining the screams of the Cali duet, aware they were off the path, tumbling, wheels over, out of control.

9

By Bolan's count there were three packs of predators to deal with. Whoever the Gatling blaster—the warrior presumed black op—if rumor panned out that American intelligence operators were sleeping with the country's worst enemies, there was no telling how far and wide their collaboration went. He'd heard about the promised sale of dual-use technology, a mystery batch of radioactive brew.

Traitors, in his mind, were the worst of cannibals. He vowed to send those who sold out their nation on their way to hell. No mercy, no exceptions.

No hope.

Then there was Cabriano and his bunch of thugs, killers, extortionists and drug dealers, to name just the short list of their crimes. From what he'd seen of the Mob pack so far, he had a pretty good picture of how they wanted life to fit for them. They were playboys, party animals, out for themselves and a good time, making sure they had plenty of dirty money in their own pockets. Fun and games came at the expense of whatever their family life. If bagged like Marelli, they were quick to want to save their own skin, ready to whine, bellyache, blame the other guy. It was the system, the wife, the judge, the lawyer who screwed them, some rat bastard did them in. It was how the wicked thought. In his estimation, the real tough guys were out there, earning an honest living, feeding a family, providing an education, trying to live right. Sometimes failing and falling down, but getting back up, not cursing their own misfortune or fate, blaming God and everyone else.

Take it on the chin, own up.

But he wouldn't find it here, on this highway to hell, among the few standing or walking wounded. No, they didn't want to give up the ghost. They wanted their idea of the good life to keep on going. The Executioner knew he couldn't allow that to happen.

The gunship had shifted. Bolan picked himself up following his tumble down the embankment. It was quite the savaging he found. Mangled red ruins of inhumanity were moaning, dragging or shimmying their zombie walk through the smoke and flames. Figure the swarm that ate them up were 12.7 mm or maybe 20 mm rounds, pounded out at anywhere from three to five thousand bites per minute. The size of the holes he found in man and machine told him they were most likely armor-piercing to boot.

The gunship was a few hundred yards north, nose dipping, slicing a new path off the road, vanishing into the woods following the direction in which one Towncar had beaten a hasty, but for the moment safe, exit. Bolan's money was on Cabriano.

A look over his shoulder, and Bolan saw no sign of Marelli. The Crown Vic was a smoking hull of fist-sized bullet holes on flattened tread. There was a good chance, he knew, the vehicle had become Marelli's hearse.

So be it.

At the moment, Bolan had a few straggling armed matters to contend with.

A hardman minus his left arm below the elbow came toward him from a pall of smoke, cursing in Spanish and shooting wildly. With a 3-round burst of autofire from his M-16, Bolan put the amputee out of his misery.

The Cali jackals, namely the Quintero Cartel, were heavily involved with this mystery deal. As the campaign unfolded—or unraveled from that point on—all indications were that a visit to Colombia was in order.

But first some mop-up was necessary.

He navigated slowly onto the road, marching his path toward the reeling cannibals, figuring five, six, tops. He was tracking the wreckage when he heard the crack of pistolfire to his rear. Wheeling, Bolan spotted Marelli, up and gunning down hardcases, pistol jumping in hand.

IT WAS THE SOUND of terror that revived Cabriano. If he never heard that damnable grind of helicopter blades again he'd...

What?

Change his ways? Promise things he could never deliver? Be faithful to his wife? Give all his money to charity? How much did he really want to live?

Plenty.

He was on his side, face mashed into glass, lip-locked on metal and vinyl, the world of horror roaring back all too soon, pondering his next move. One—no, two—voices were cutting through that awful bleating, hollering something in Spanish. He looked up, wondering about his own injuries, the squall blowing glass in his face, when rolling thunder severed what was already an ungodly din. Whatever Hildago and the wheel-man had been screaming went with them, as Cabriano found some of their remains splatter the broken teeth of the passenger window.

He began digging for hardware, fingers wrapping around the pistol, when he spotted the faceless creature in the window.

"I thought I told you not to run, Petey."

He almost had the pistol out but froze a heartbeat too long, terrified by the helmeted, visored apparition. Before he knew it, a hand that felt the size of a small car came down, had him by the hair.

"I thought I told you there was nothing to be scared of?"

Cabriano felt terror hold down the scream, as he was hauled through the window. He heard the voice of doom growl, "You don't listen too good, do you, ass-hole?"

MARELLI CONSIDERED himself a take charge, action kind of guy. That in mind he couldn't quite see himself just stand around, thumb up his butt, letting the big guy do all the dirty work for him—no, have all the fun. For one thing, the SOBs on hand had come to check him out of the world. Under normal circumstances that alone would be enough for him to dive into the fray, take enough pounds of flesh to fill a slaughterhouse.

But there was nothing normal about the big man, or the moment.

Marelli had the trooper's pistol, was marching down the line of cars, an image of a huge white shark leaping to mind the more he observed the bruiser wading into all the blood and guts. No fear, no hesitation, the big shooter just eating them up, fast, furious, no mercy. It was awkward, wielding the pistol with hands bound by plastic cuffs, but adrenaline took over.

And there were still a few walking wounded reeling about, looking for payback, howling from the smoke and flames, not wanting to give up the ghost.

Then there was the bite of leaking gas in his nose, the fear one of the vehicles would ignite, incineration a definite concern.

Time, he figured, to wrap it up before he was federal toast.

Marelli started picking targets, the man-eater on the far side, M-16 blazing. Each vehicle was turned into a hearse, as he devoured whatever life cried out from behind ruined windshields. Two gory stick figures washed in blood, head to toe, staggered into view, partly obscured by drifting smoke. Marelli tapped the trigger twice, opting for head shots. The big man wheeled on him.

"Drop the weapon!"

Marelli hesitated, ready to argue. Hell, if he'd wanted to he could have already tagged himself a man-eater, and to be honest with himself the thought had crossed his mind. Then what? He figured he was better off at that point, safer at any rate, with the man-eater.

"I won't tell you again!"

Marelli threw away the pistol and thrust his hands up as the warrior came his way. "Hey, I was only lookin' to help, pal."

The man's look told Marelli he didn't need any assistance.

Marelli checked the highway, amazed no traffic had appeared in either direction. The big guy was off, inspecting their Crown Vic, Marelli telling him, "Don't bother. Radiator's shot to hell for one thing, but I guess you can see the steam."

The big guy swept over to him and took him by the arm.

"Next time I see you holding a gun will be your last."

Marelli was already a believer.

ROLLINS HAD ALREADY LEFT the building. An emergency meeting had been demanded by the attorney general, and he knew his AWOL status would raise eyebrows, and ire. The feces was hitting the fan, from D.C. to the Catskills.

Trouble was, he suspected he was already sunk.

He decided to hit a pub on K Street for a quick belt or two, get his head together, sort through his options.

Which, he already feared, were nonexistent.

Looking over his shoulder, eyeballing each passing face, jumping as a horn blared, he recalled the most dreaded words he could remember hearing in his life.

"Mr. Brognola is coming around. His vitals have stabilized, and it appears he keeps trying to say something."

Rollins had nearly shrieked at the agent posted to watch Brognola. "What?"

"Sounds like he's trying to say a name."

There was only one name Rollins could imagine Brognola struggling to blurt out.

He barged into the pub, beelined for the bar. Checking his watch, he found there was plenty of time to clean out his bank account, race home, gather up his passport, empty out the safe in his room. He would skip the country, vanish into thin air. Change identities, of course, a man with a little money could set up pretty decent, he heard, in the lower Americas. Spread a little grease around…

Run, then—that made the most sense.

He heard the bartender repeat the question of what he wanted. He ordered a double Scotch, neat. The guy held his ground for a second too long. Why the evil eye? he wondered, searching the bar, the booths next, knowing damn well his paranoia about phantoms was well founded. The drink came back, guy asking if he wanted a menu.

Rollins shook his head. "I won't be staying."

"You having a bad day, mister?"

"I'm having a bad life."

Rollins turned away from the measured look, grateful to be alone. Images of the ex-gunnery sergeant boiled to mind, but he'd checked in with Worthy before vacating the premises. Figure he'd bought himself an hour or so head start.

Killing the drink and ordering another, Rollins checked his surroundings again. He hated the nagging suspicion he was being shadowed. Maybe Brognola wouldn't make it. Maybe he'd lapse into a coma. Maybe he'd fled too soon.

No, he told himself, he was making the right choice. To stay and face the music was a sure death sentence. Run, and keep on running.

BOLAN GAVE UP DIGGING through the mangled ruins of the bodies heaped near the Towncar dumped on its side. A few close rounds during the heat of combat, one of which had shot his own cell phone off his hip...

No time to curse misfortune.

"Now what?" he heard Marelli ask.

"Now, we walk and rustle up a ride."

Marelli chuckled. "You realize what we must look like to some tree huggers out here?"

"I'm a federal agent, in case you forgot."

"I don't know what you are..."

Bolan jacked Marelli by the arm, shoving him down what appeared to be a footpath. He needed wheels, a phone. With Brognola clinging to life the soldier had to count on Price to clean up whatever trap had been laid for him in all this mess.

Ears tuned to the bleat of rotor blades or sirens in their wake, Bolan saw the Winnebago, parked in a clearing. He ushered more speed out of Marelli, closing on the RV. He hung the M-16 around his shoulder and dug out his Justice Department credentials. There was no sign of life as he crept closer, then he saw an elderly man step around the front side.

"Relax," Bolan told him, flashing his wallet ID, worried the old guy might have a heart attack, the way he threw his arms up, lips quivering. "I'm with the Justice Department."

RICHARD GROGEN WAS SICK and tired of the mobsters being all in a snit every time he turned around. He had worries of his own, enough so that the coming chore would lighten the mental burden a little.

Maybe.

The black op DOD airfield was tucked away in a stretch of remote desert in southeast Utah. The sun was breaking over a lunar landscape, Grogen already feeling the first beads of sweat moisten his forehead. He was anxious to be on his way. One look at the black cargo gunship, one ear tuned to Gagliano's pissing and moaning how come his guys were doing all the mule work, and Grogen gave his new orders a mental kicking around.

The drums of toxin were already rolled into the

cargo bay of the big bird, fastened down with enough strap to contain King Kong.

Or so he hoped.

He was ordered to ride with the cargo to the end of the line. Gagliano and his men were being cut loose. And woe be unto him, he knew, if he didn't carry out those orders. Disobedience meant termination in his racket, and that didn't mean picking up a pink slip at the end of the day's business.

Marching out of the office, he looked at the hangar, a slew of curses lashing his ears. The new team along for the ride had been beefed up to an eight-man force. Apparently their first stop was Miami. Touchdown in Homestead, then they were off and running and gunning to pick up this much-ballyhooed and dreaded disk, the one the hit man had created such a furor with.

He gave the big beast—tagged the Flying Shark—a long once-over, as Gagliano flailed about, huffing and puffing. Built to DOD specs, it was a hybrid cross between a C-130 and a Spectre gunship, complete with all the firepower. All avionics and sensors were upgraded to supertech but…

It was those damn drums. Say some heavy turbulence jostled them around, lead shield or not, he knew that garbage was a thousand times more potent than acid. It could burn through just about any alloy known to man.

The markings on the drums gave him pause, too. Inside a triangle there was an octagon and a pentagon, all entwined at various angles. Spooky. He'd be damned if he knew what all that meant.

Grogen found his troops assembled, half behind the Mob force, the other half staggered beside him. Ready to do the deed.

"All set?" he asked Gagliano.

"Yeah. No thanks to you."

He looked at Henson, who gave him the nod. "Battened down, sir."

Grogen, unslinging the HK subgun, gave his troops his own nod.

The mobsters didn't stand a chance, as they were hemmed in, front to back, fat cattle ripe for the slaughter. Eight subguns cut loose in unison, sweeping the hoods, stem to stern. They screamed, cursed, were shredded to red ruins, dead on their feet.

Apparently, Grogen thought, as the last thug dropped, there were too many problems in New York to trust Cabriano any longer. Not that they ever did, but the intent now was to squeeze the last piece of useful life out of the crime boss.

Grogen held his ground, staring at the Flying Shark. Beyond Miami, he knew they weren't exactly going to the land of milk and honey.

Colombia.

Down there, he knew it could all get real dicey.

He heard the heavy trundle of wheels over hard-packed earth, watched as the black van rolled up and braked near the strewed corpses.

"Let's be quick about this, gentlemen," he ordered his men, as the first few bodies were hefted off the ground and dumped in the van.

One look at the smoke pluming from the stack jutting from the far edge of the big hangar, and he knew the incinerator was already fired up.

"I FIGURED YOU for a runner. Going gets a little tough, you were ready to bail on us all along."

Rollins was standing by the wall safe when he heard the strange voice from behind. He froze, heart in his throat, then felt himself choke down the sob. One second he was grabbing cash with lightning fast cobra strikes, about to be home free, the next moment he had the voice of doom in his ear. For a brief moment he wrestled with two options. Buy, or shoot his way out.

"I wouldn't do what you're thinking."

Rollins couldn't find the courage to turn and face the stranger. "Who are you? FBI? Justice?"

"Nope. Let's just say I work for the people who actually run this country, or pull the string behind the scenes."

"You're black ops, in other words."

"Helped put together this whole deal. From Brognola to Cabriano to the Cali Cartel. By the way, Brognola came awake long enough to finger you. I apologize if I caused you unnecessary grief by not finishing the job."

Rollins cursed. "Why?"

"Why what?"

"What's it all about?"

"National security."

"You're telling me a crime boss, Brognola and Cooper are a threat to national security?"

"More than you could ever understand."

Rollins felt his hand shake, gauged the distance to the voice. He was finished, but the more he thought about it now, the more insane it had sounded before he ever accepted the first payoff. "Who are they?"

"We don't know, well, not exactly, but we've had suspicions now for some years they're part of a covert agency not even those silly pukes on the Hill know about."

"I can pay you to let me walk out of here."

"Pay me? My friend, I'm going to take back the money anyway."

The laughter told Rollins everything he needed to know.

"This thing was never about you, Rollins. It's about Cabriano, a shadow deal we cut with him."

"The deal with the Cali Cartel and terrorists."

"That would be the one. See, we intend to take the whole damn lot of them down, all parties gathered, one big happy family. There will be a ton or two of cash on hand, some will go into black ops coffers to fight the war on terrorism and the war on drugs."

"And let me guess where a fat chunk of change will go."

"Hey, there's some of us paid some heavy dues along the way, friend. We're not cut-and-run types like you."

Rollins thought he was going to be sick, the bastard standing there, laughing at him, no way out.

"Back or front, Rollins?"

"Why?" he cried.

"Because you're a loser. We gave you a chance to

prove otherwise, but you caved at the worst time. Now, I'm left cleaning up messes all over the map."

Loser, huh? Rollins thought. The guy was saying something he didn't hear, his ears roaring with hate and fury. He was wheeling, pistol out, but he knew he'd never make it.

10

Beyond feeling as if he'd been launched back in time to star in an episode of *The Twilight Zone,* Cabriano had a frightening picture of the future taking shape in his head the longer he sat in the silent presence of the three armed men in black.

He had a pretty good notion who these nameless faceless specters were, and he admitted to himself the spaceman scared the crap out of him. He was the shooter with the big gun, after all, still wearing the helmet with visor that hid his face. Like some proud papa he stood there beside that mammoth Gatling gun, hauled back minutes ago on some electronically controlled section of the floor. The hatchway then slid shut, killing sunlight, leaving the glowing halo of monitors and his rising fears. It was as if, Cabriano thought, he was itching to start spraying again, even inside the tight confines of the chopper.

They had dumped him like he was nothing more than a sack of garbage in some draped webbing he figured passed for their idea of a seat. Cabriano wished they'd say something. While they studied him like some

exotic bug under a microscope, he looked at the walls—
bulkheads, he believed was the accurate military term.
They sort of created a dome overhead, bubbles pock-
ing the walls, weird, like he was on a spaceship.

Cabriano felt he was, indeed, trapped in another di-
mension.

"Smoke?"

He jerked his head, the spaceman coming to him, offering him a butt. "Yeah, thanks."

Maybe this would be all right, after all, he thought.
So what if they wasted the cream of his soldiers. Cali
would never know what happened on the road, since he
was the only survivor. All this death and mayhem since
last night, and he was still breathing.

Still there was something he didn't trust about the
moment. He hesitated, then reached out to accept the
peace offering when the fist slammed him in the mouth.
"What did you do that for?" he hollered at the crew-cut
black-clad shooter standing beside him. Then he looked
to the spaceman, as if for an explanation, spit blood on
the floorboard and took another shot to the kisser.

"Don't spit on my chopper, asshole."

Instead of handing him the smoke, the spaceman
gave it to his hitter.

"Who the fuck are you guys?"

"I think you already know."

"Yeah," Cabriano snarled, tasted the blood filling up
his mouth and dripping down his throat. "Military black
ops, maybe Special Forces."

"Oh, we're special, all right."

"Means you can run amok all over the countryside, wasting honest citizens."

He took yet another fist to the teeth.

"Goddammit!"

"Don't curse," the spaceman warned. "Don't get smart. Your life depends on the cooperation we receive in the next twenty-four hours or so."

"Cooperate doing what?"

"The deal with the Colombians is in motion. You're going to help during the transaction."

Cabriano felt his jaw drop. Blood began trickling down his chin, so he wiped it off with the back of his hand. "I thought that was my deal."

"Not anymore. You've been having a lot of difficulties the past twenty-four hours. You couldn't even see to it Marelli handed over the disk."

"I was working on it."

"So were we. And we already know where it is."

When they fell silent, Cabriano quietly asked, "You gonna tell me, or is it some big government secret?"

"It's in Miami. Marelli's girlfriend, Tina, the stripper? Ever hear of her?"

"Vaguely."

Spaceman chuckled. "That's the problem here, Petey. You haven't been watching the store so well. Something this important, the whole deal with my people worked with you through Marelli and Big Tony, could expose critical national security matters. And we end up doing all the grunt work for you."

"I've got soldiers in Miami. I do a lot of business down there."

"You're out of that part of it. And your so-called soldiers get in our way, well at the rate it's been going for you, pretty soon you'll be hiring punks off street corners."

"I don't get this, none of it."

"Yours is not to understand why."

Cabriano wanted to fly into a rage, but good business sense took over. "All this big cooperation I'm giving you, you bulling your way into my end of it…"

"Ah, yes, money." Spaceman chuckled.

Cabriano took smoke in the face. "Well?"

"You really think, with the cargo—which, by the way, will already be there, and which, by the way, my people technically own—someone is just going to hand you a bunch of money and say have a nice day?"

Cabriano grimaced when another cloud hit him in the eyes. "This ain't right. My end was ten million on delivery. Ten more for the next shipment."

"Let me tell you something. I could hand you a C-note right now, and tell you to take a hike."

"Meaning you don't think you need me. You got all the good stuff, old Peter can kiss your collective asses. You're in tight with the Quinteros."

"Up to a point, we need you. Maybe we're looking to take down the Quinteros, put our people in to rule the cartel. Maybe hand you the keys to their kingdom when the smoke clears."

"You're nuts. You're government agents of some type. Not drug dealers."

Spaceman chuckled. "What you don't know about how the real world works is a lot. The war on terrorism has grabbed center stage, the war on drugs has taken a back seat. We control the flow of narcotics, we can control the terrorists."

Cabriano couldn't believe what he was hearing. "Why are you doing this to me?"

"Listen to yourself. This isn't and never was about you, Petey. To answer your question, though, it's because I don't like you. You're criminal scum. All you want is to keep on living like a big shot. Play ball, you'll come out of this okay."

"I guess I don't need to ask what happens if I don't. I sleep with the fishes."

Spaceman laughed. "You're smarter than I thought, Petey. You answered your own question."

"Okay, okay. I'll go the distance on this." Cabriano felt his hand shaking. For the first time he could recall he was on his own, his life in the hands of others—men he didn't even know—and he was scared to death.

"You want that smoke now, Petey?"

He thought about it, almost shook his head, but Spaceman had one out.

"Go on. Now that we have an understanding."

Cabriano held his hand out, ashamed of the shaking. He took the smoke, waiting for another hammer to the jaw but it never came.

"Hey, like I told you a while back. Nothing to be afraid of, now that we're in business together. Cheer up."

FBI SAC JEFF TIMMER didn't have the first clue as to what the hell he was looking at, much less armed with a ready answer to hand to the director. Oh, he'd heard stories from other agents who fought in wars overseas, the gory details of combat sometimes leaking out in conversation after a few rounds of drinks, leaving him to wonder how much of the talk came out of the bottle. Ten years on the job, one of the youngest SACs in the Bureau, and he'd never fired the first shot in anger, and now...

The carnage he'd found, from the Justice safehouse to a stretch of highway a few miles south—not counting the corpses that littered the woods—left him speechless.

He knew he had the cell phone pressed to his ear, the director on the other end wanting a full report, but he was numb, dead.

This was a scene he expected to find more in Baghdad or the Gaza Strip than on American soil.

It was his show now, either way. The full weight of the state police and the FBI were behind him. The skies were swarming with helicopters, the highway cordoned off by troopers, meat wagons on the crime scene, body bags rolling out. But, from the look of the damage to the dead—what with arms, legs, feet chewed off and scattered around four vehicles riddled with so many bullet holes, one of the rigs mangled to scrap by what appeared to him a rocket-propelled grenade—there was no way to figure out what parts belonged to which body.

No ID on any of the victims. No eyewitnesses. Two more bodies strewed near a Towncar in the woods shot to hell and dumped in a gully.

To say the investigation was a mystery—a nightmare—gave him pause to consider a career change.

"Timmer! I'm talking to you."

"Sir, I'm here," he answered, wandering up and down the line of vehicular trash, veering away from an amputated leg.

"Any sign of Cooper?"

"No, sir, but AD Rollins gave us a description, confirmed by Justice agents assigned to the man's detail in Brooklyn. We have an APB, BOLOS, roadblocks from here to—"

"Forget Cooper."

"Sir?"

"You got shit in your ears, son? Cooper is not behind this fiasco—at least not what started this mess."

"But, sir, AD Rollins said—"

"Forget Rollins."

"Sir?"

"Stop sirring me, son, you're starting to really piss me off."

"Yes."

"Rollins is dead. He went AWOL this morning, just before Brognola fingered him as the one who walked him into an ambush."

"I don't understand."

"I don't have a lot of time to explain. Rollins was shot in his home. Open safe, passport by his body, assailant unknown, but I've got a house full of those at the moment. He was getting ready, or trying, to leave behind this horror show he helped to engineer. I suspect Peary was his inside man. And this all tracks back to Cabriano somehow."

"Speaking of the Mob, Marelli's vanished." Feeling he had an opening to take charge and shine, Timmer laid out all the aerial and ground sweeps underway, roadblocks. He thought he was on a roll, ready to barge ahead when the director interrupted him.

"That's nice."

Timmer, considering the slaughter he had to figure out, couldn't believe how calm—or perhaps sarcastic—the director sounded. He choked back the "sir" in question form.

"Keep at it, Timmer. I'm sending more people to assist with the investigation. Forensic teams, more manpower and so forth. Right now, if you run into Cooper, you treat him like you would your own beloved father. I'm in the process of calling off the wolves on him."

"With all due respect, Director, there's evidence pointing to Cooper as being the one-man army that nearly burned down half of Brooklyn last night."

"Right. You check with NYPD?"

"Well…I…"

"If you do, you'll find the only property damage, the only bodies that may or may not belong to Cooper had Cabriano all over them."

"Are you telling me, Director, the Justice Department is in the business of declaring war on organized crime? Carte blanche? License to kill?"

"Far as that goes, I don't know what to tell you. Do the best you can up there, but my orders to you are to fairly kiss Cooper's ass if you run into him. We clear on that?"

"Yes, sir."

"Any more questions?"

"No, Director."

"Then get back to work."

When the line went dead, Timmer felt as if the air had been punched from his lungs. He shook his head, stared at the carnage.

"What the hell is going on here? Who the hell is Cooper?" he asked the dead.

WHEN THE GOOD NEWS KEPT rolling in, Bolan felt his hackles rise. In his world there was always bad news waiting just around the next bend, usually armed, usually angry and looking for his scalp. Even still it was relief, if only for the moment, to know hope was alive and well, at least in the person of Hal Brognola.

The warrior's second call to Barbara Price, patched through by a series of cutouts, was placed when they had put the Manhattan skyline an hour or so behind them. They were rolling south in the borrowed Winnebago belonging to Mr. And Mrs. Degan. Bolan watched the highway unfold, perched close to the elderly couple, with Marelli on his flank. He was grateful the Degans weren't the nervous kind, both of them pledging full cooperation, Bolan sensing they were grateful for a little adventure or believing they were helping their country, or both. They had declined financial compensation, but Bolan decided he'd take their address, just the same, make sure they received an early Christmas cash gift.

As previously instructed by the Farm's mission controller, they were headed in the direction of Baltimore. Price was arranging a classified military flight from an airfield sometimes used by Stony Man. A blacksuit crew of three would be on hand to assist Bolan.

"I know you called in some heavy markers on this one," he told Price.

"You don't know the half of it."

"Tell me all about it when it's over."

"Count on it. I got the heat off you, and next to Hal being on the mend, that's the best news. No APBs. You're off the hook with every law-enforcement agency across the country. Still, since we don't know who or what the late Rollins was in bed with, to be on the safe side finish the mission as Colonel Brandon Stone. That cover will clear you with the DEA in Miami and Cali. I'm juggling a couple more markers to get you contacts in Cali, specifically DEA who can get you cleared with Colombian authorities."

"Let me take care of the next stop first. The way this campaign has shaped up…" Bolan paused.

"Understood. What are your plans for Marelli?"

Bolan glanced at the hit man, who looked a little sulky about something. "I'll take my witness with me to the next stop, then when I have in hand what everyone's been after, I'll turn him over to our people."

He heard Marelli curse, adding something about him being a Judas bastard, then Bolan growled at the hit man, "Watch your filthy mouth."

"I take it after all the excitement in the Catskills The Butcher is having second thoughts about being in the WPP?" Price asked.

"Nervous and worried, but it's under control."

"I guess you offered him the same sweetheart deal that's been on the table for steering you in the right direction of the disk?"

"Against my better judgment."

"You'd just as soon shoot him as spend another wonderful moment with him?"

"You know me all too well."

Price chuckled on the other end. "Okay, you're good to land on the other end at Opa-Locka Airfield. There will be ground transportation waiting."

"One other thing," Bolan said. "Any chance of getting our own people to watch our man? Laid up like he is, with agents we don't know, I'd hate to see anything happen to him after what he's been through."

"I get the picture. I can work on it, make some calls, but no promises."

"If you get too much resistance on that front, find out who's throwing up the wall."

"Will do, but my clout at the department has limits. If that falls through, I can slip in one of our own people, a concerned long-lost cousin to keep an eye on Hal."

"That'll work, if all else fails," Bolan said.

"All intelligence you'll need on the Quintero Cartel and their Mideast friends will be waiting for you with our people. Fact is, we should have gone after them a long time ago. Beyond narcotics they've cornered the market, it appears, on getting at least dirty bombs into the hands of fanatics."

"We're here now. And the way it's shaking out, I can drop more buzzards than the cartel." Bolan listened to the pause on the other end, aware of the anxious hours that lay ahead for Price, the Stony Man team and Brognola's family.

"Striker, the hell of this is, we may never know who paid off whom, how far or wide this conspiracy reaches. It galls me to think a few snakes may slither off to strike another day."

"Unfortunately, it happens. We both know that. That's why I take it one snake at a time. If they slip away today, they'll crawl out from under another rock tomorrow."

There was another moment of silence, then Price said, "Touch back with me when you're in the air, in case of any more breaking news."

"Will do. If there's a chance, get word to our friend he's in my thoughts."

"I can pass that along."

Bolan punched off and offered a quick silent prayer for the full recovery of the big Fed. Marelli interrupted his thoughts.

"What's the deal, pal?"

Bolan turned to look at the hit man. "What?"

"The deal, I still got my deal? All that cloak-and-dagger yak-yak didn't exactly fill my heart with hope. Yes or no, I still got my deal?"

Bolan drilled a cold stare into the hit man. There it was, he thought, but why should he expect anything different? Tough guy, decades of dipping his hands in blood. Who knew how much innocent blood he'd shed, families he'd ruined? His marker was way overdue, and all he could think of was saving himself, getting his way, the angry child. He turned away, rose.

"You're gonna fuckin' Judas me, ain't ya, you rotten son of a—"

Bolan wheeled and hammered a backhand fist into Marelli's mouth. "One more word before we step off this rig, and your deal dies. Don't speak, just nod, if you understand."

Marelli ignored the blood dripping off his chin, and nodded.

Bolan went to the Degans and felt the tension from the elderly couple. He handed Mrs. Degan the cell phone and told her, "Sorry about that. He won't be any more trouble."

"No problem," Mrs. Degan said.

Bolan saw a strange twinkle light up the old man's eyes as he said, "You're fine with us. Looks like you can handle just about anything."

"What he's saying," Mrs. Degan added, smiling, "is we trust you. We know good people when we see them. You won't let any harm come to us. Now that one back there," she added in a near whisper, "he's bad. Whatever he's done, something tells me he's getting off too easy."

Bolan nodded. "Ma'am, believe me when I tell you, no truer words could you have ever spoken."

11

Tony Bartino hated Miami. Forget the heat and humidity, the fact he had to change shirts four times a day. Forget the traffic, car or mammal, hell he was from New York City, after all. The foreigners, why that was just part of any city zooscape, and they were just a good reason anyway to keep his .45 on his person at all times, in case he had to go Charlie Bronson on the spot. Truth be told he had, three times, but that's why they had the Glades and gators a short drive west, he figured. Why, too, he kept a few cops on his payroll.

No. What really bugged him was the crime down here. Turn on the tube, and every day there was a rash of senseless murders, rapes and robberies that would make the toughest New Yorker wince. Sure, tourists grabbed the headlines, carjackings and such, but he knew of giant corporations that had pulled up stakes down here because of all the animals. Of course, he knew Miami was still high on coke, thanks to both the Cabriano Family and the Quintero Cartel. Almost without exception he also knew all this brutality was fueled by the very product he dumped on the streets. In his mind, though, if they couldn't afford it or didn't know when to say when, don't do it in the first damn place.

End of discussion.

So, why did he stay? Easy. The broads, the strip joints, not to mention he was something of a big shot in South Beach, often filmed by paparazzi being ogled by movie and rock stars, damn near fawned over in some cases, script writers begging to do his life story, wanting to put *GoodFellas* to shame.

Then there was the money and personal ambition to consider. Being the Don's frontline capo down here, who helped all the moving and shaking between the Quinteros, their bankers, offshore and otherwise—well, there was the future to think about.

That's why this Marelli nonsense as of late had him clamoring to be more, to climb higher, to secure the future. Tough guy turned stoolie, after something like a hundred hits under his belt. He never did like the SOB.

If the guy did sing, they were all screwed. But, if in fact this disk, which allegedly laid out all the Family secrets even beyond the Quinteros, existed…

There it was.

Get the disk, take it to Cabriano and hand it to him personally. Might as well knight him before the whole crew of soldiers, from Miami to New York, the Don's favored son.

And Bartino knew where to begin looking. Truth was, the more he'd thought about it the past two days, the more sense it made. It was always the girlfriend who

knew everything, or had in her possession anything of
value a man owned. Wise guy or not, it was a fact as
old as Adam and Eve. What bothered him was he hadn't
thought of it before now.

The gentlemen's club was called Rocco's. Named
after the owner, Frankie Rocco, who laundered fat
chunks of cash through the club. It was tucked near a
strip mall in Coral Gables, just south of the airport.

It was damn thoughtful of Tina, Bartino thought,
that she'd run her mouth to a fellow dancer about holding on to something huge for her boyfriend.

Bingo.

He could have gone through the kitchen or service
door, but in a way this was his joint, and which of these
broads could possibly manage to make it through the
night without at least laying eyes on him? Leave Garpo
to sit in the Towncar in the back parking lot, since
they'd be hauling Tina out the service door. He loved
his grand entrances.

He waited while Calebria held the door, Carmine on
his left flank. Bartino saw a funny look fall over Calebria's craggy mug. "What?"

"I don't know, Tony," he said, checking the front lot,
then searching the wide boulevard of pink shops and
boutiques.

"What don't you know?"

"It don't feel right. I got this itch in my back, like
we're bein' followed."

"The only itch you got is between your legs, 'cause
you don't get laid enough."

"We should've run this by the boss. And don't you find it weird we ain't heard from New York the last day? Guys are like clocks up there, always callin' down, checkin' the store."

"Listen to me, both of you," Bartino growled, glancing at Carmine, who was now doing a phantom search of his own. "The boss put me in charge of things in Miami while you two were still up north shaking down bookies. He don't call, means he's busy. Now. Can we do this?"

Bartino shook his head, laughing as the door was held wide. "You guys."

BOLAN COULDN'T QUITE imagine the fine upstanding, middle- to upper-class citizenry of ritzy Coral Gables caring too much for a Mobbed-up strip joint planted in their midst. But, stranger things happened, and the warrior could pretty much picture the greasing of skid, or the blackmail dialogue that went on behind the public political podium.

What wasn't news in the least was that a social-security number and driver's license could not only track down an individual, but could give anyone with time and interest enough information to unravel their life story.

Welcome to the age of Big Brother. Bolan gave Price and the cybersleuths at the Farm a mental salute.

Of course, Marelli knew her work schedule by heart, but since he'd taken a wake-up call to the teeth, and was looking mean and sullen during the whole flight to

Opa-Locka, Bolan had him call Rocco's, to double-check if Tina, a.k.a. Starr was dancing that night.

The fluke came when Bolan spotted Tony Bartino and sidekicks stroll through the front doors. He had his blacksuit wheelman navigate their van in the direction from which the threesome had come. A roll down the service alley, and Bolan spotted Bartino's Towncar in what appeared to be a small employee parking lot, flanked by palm trees. The Towncar faced the back end of the club, the driver dangling an arm out the window, working on a cigarette.

"Keep driving," Bolan ordered. "Park it where that Towncar's driver can't see you."

A perfect cubbyhole loomed at the edge of a pink stucco building. The blacksuit eased around the corner, braking.

Mentally Bolan ran through his options. Have a chat at gunpoint with the smoker, or roll into the club with two of his three blacksuits, or wait for Bartino and trail him. Bolan believed Bartino had figured out the girl had the disk. But knowing the thug's track record for murder, extortion and drug trafficking, to name a few of his crimes, smart money told him they'd take her for a ride.

Bolan had shed full combat regalia for the Miami leg. Beneath the loose-fitting black windbreaker, though, the reliable Beretta 93-R with attached sound suppressor hung under his left armpit, a mini-Uzi under the right, the .44 Magnum Desert Eagle riding his right hip and two frag grenades in coat pockets rounding out the arsenal.

"Now what?" Marelli growled from the back, sand-wiched between the other two blacksuits. "We sit here, thumbs up our butts?"

"No, that's still your department, Marelli," Bolan told the hit man.

"How do you like that?" Marelli grumbled. "All I done for you, all I'm doin' for you now. Smack me in the mouth, treat me like a punk. No respect."

"I know," Bolan said. "What's the world coming to?"

Already understood by his blacksuits he would raise them by TAC radio only in a pinch, the Executioner opened the door and stepped into the hot Miami night.

Time to meet Tony Bartino, just another shade, Bolan knew, of The Butcher.

"I DON'T KNOW ANYTHING about any damn disk!"

Bartino loved it when they lied. It made working on them that much more fun, broads in particular. Already he was conjuring up pictures of what he would do to her. Oh, she would give up the disk, but he had half the night beyond that to make her forget all about her bull-shit boyfriend hit man legend.

Trailing his soldier for the service door, Bartino kept a tight grip on Tina's arm, checking out the whole pack-age. She was a looker, no doubt about it, black pumps accentuating long taut tanned legs, white panties hugging an apple rump, a frilly lace top holding back the melons. The face could have belonged to a model, topped off by natural blond hair, though he couldn't be sure about that until he took a peek. That would come soon enough.

"You tellin' me, Tina baby, Rachel and Frankie had it all wrong?"

"Damn straight they do."

As Carmine thrust open the door, Bartino manhandled his plaything into the lot. He found his driver enjoying a smoke, lost in thought. "Goddammit, Jackie, stop beatin' off. Get the car started."

His troops falling in beside him, he was checking the lot when he saw the figure in black weaving through the palm trees. Great, he thought, watching as the guy fumbled a pack of cigarettes, staggering their way, a drunken bum, probably wanting a light.

"Hey," Bartino heard the guy say. "Anybody got a light?"

"Get lost!" Bartino snarled, angling for the Towncar.

"Hey, mister…all I want…"

Bartino couldn't believe this nonsense. His future in the Cabriano Family was, quite literally, in his hands. Walking out the door with his ticket to a bigger tomorrow, and a drunk was going to force him to make a scene. Was upper-crust Coral Gables going down the toilet like the rest of Miami?

"Goddammit, take a hike, you drunk, before I kick your ass all the way back into your mama's womb!"

Bartino was thinking the guy didn't listen too good, or was too juiced on booze, when a warning bell began ringing in his skull. He pulled back on Tina, guts coiling.

The answer came a fraction of a second too late. Bulges beneath the windbreaker were the initial tip-off, then there was the sudden shift in attitude, a feral look in the big man in black's eye that told him this was an act all along.

The who, what and why shelved, Bartino was clawing for his .45 when the first two burps hit the air from the big guy's way. Carmine and Calebria were crying out, toppling before he cleared leather. He heard Tina scream, his ticket to greatness thrashing in his hold when the big guy, moving like a flash of lightning, chugged out two more bullets. Glass shattering, Bartino snatched a look toward the Towncar. Garpo's face rammed the steering wheel, a black spray hitting the windshield. Whoever the mystery shooter, Bartino knew when some bastard had come knocking to punch his ticket. Animal reflex took over, as he locked an arm around Tina's throat, choking off her scream. The .45 was out, the big guy rolling on like a wraith of doom, Bartino tracking, shouting, "Back off!"

He was about to embellish the threat, the muzzle of his .45 up and pressed to Tina's skull, when he heard that awful chug, and the lights snapped off.

"SIR, WE HAVE A PROBLEM."

"I don't want to hear about problems."

There was a long pause on the other end, Grogen silently cursing the dead air, the TAC radio with secured frequency suddenly trembling in his hand.

"Well?" Grogen asked.

"Sir, we have an unidentified player who just terminated Bartino and three of his soldiers, and took the girl.

A big guy, sir, from our surveillance. I would say he was a professional of some type, probably military."

"One of us you're trying to say?"

"It wasn't as if I had the chance to have a conversation with the man, sir."

"You're in no position, mister, to get a smart tongue."

"Yes, sir. He used a Beretta with sound suppressor, so that furthers suspicion he's more than maybe a Cabriano rival. The van in which they left the scene is similar in make and color to ours, with a satellite dish I would assume is for tracking, perhaps intercepting police bans. I ran the plates, civilian, but—"

"But nothing turned up on your trace. Limbo. Dead end."

Which told Grogen a covert unknown had jumped into the picture.

"Sir, we are presently tailing their vehicle."

"Head count?"

"Undetermined. The unidentified, the female target and driver that we know of."

Grogen felt his blood pressure rise, his heart thundering in his ears. He began pacing in the office, glaring down into the hangar, dreading bad news more than he did the cargo being guarded by the other half of his eight-man team.

"You were supposed to have grabbed the girl," he said, checking his watch, "an hour ago. Explain yourself."

"We were pulled over by a policeman in Coconut Grove."

"What? You gotta be shitting me!" he exploded. The rare outburst briefly made him think he'd been spending too much time with low-life hoods, his usual cold professional demeanor contaminated by the company he'd kept.

"A taillight was out."

If the mission wasn't so serious, poised now to spiral into the abyss, Grogen would have laughed. Only in Miami, he thought, the drug capital of the country, would a cop stop a vehicle for the flimsiest of reasons. Unbelievable.

"And I bet you're going to tell me," Grogen said, "he pulled his weapon, wanted the four of you to step out of the vehicle when he saw your hardware."

"The government plates, our bogus DOD credentials should have kept the incident from happening."

Grogen choked on his rage. "Are you telling me you were forced to dispatch him?"

"I'm afraid we had to, sir."

"Any witnesses?"

"I can't say for absolute certainty, sir."

This was no time to come unhinged, Grogen knew, and any damage control was now gone with a dead Miami cop.

"It would appear, sir, they are now heading in the direction of the female target's condominium on Bayshore."

"You have half an hour to complete the mission or abort. Check back in thirty minutes. Given your situation, all resistance from this point on is to be dispatched. You copy?" Grogen said.

"Roger."

Grogen marched out of the office, seething. They needed to be wheels up, ten, fifteen minutes ago if they were to stick to schedule. Four of his best shooters, sent out on what should have been an easy task, and now they had a dead cop, a mystery shooter on the loose, who may or may not be black ops, and...

What next?

The flight to Cali, even riding nearly on top of the radioactive stew, was suddenly looking preferable to finding his team getting snapped up by MPD, or engaging local cops in what would prove a suicide stand, at best. Either way, Grogen knew a bloodbath, maybe even a hurricane of slaughter, was about to hit Miami.

Time to bail, he decided. They didn't need the disk that bad. Not when he considered the bottom line, or weighed the risk of personal exposure.

12

"Jimmy, what kind of jackpot have you put me in? What the hell is going on here? Are these some more of your hoodlum buddies, like Bartino and the others that guy gunned down?"

"Look, Tina, all you gotta do, just give this guy the disk, keep your mouth shut…"

"Keep my mouth shut? I nearly had my head blown off back there!"

Despite his previous warning, Bolan was again forced to put an end to their romantic reunion. He twisted in the shotgun seat, pinned them both with an icy stare. "Both of you, be quiet, cooperate, obey me, and you might leave Miami breathing."

"Breathing? Obey you? Leave Miami? Jimmy, what's he talking about leave Miami?"

Bolan had other problems than playing referee to their squabbling. He checked his sideglass, found the same nearly identical black van, still shadowing their bumper, four car lengths or so back, as they navigated north against the glittering resort skyline of hotels and condos in Bayshore.

"Jimmy, I'm not leaving Miami, I'm not—"

"Listen to me," Bolan growled at the woman. "Men are coming to kill you. They want the disk. Your options are slim and none unless you hand me the disk, then enter, at least temporarily, the Witness Protection Program."

"The what? You gotta be kidding me! I'm no gangster."

"No," Bolan told her. "What you are is in deep trouble if you don't do what I say when I say."

He held her look, Marelli giving his woman the nod.

"How far, Marelli?" Bolan asked.

"Comin' up another few blocks. You got someone on your tail, don't you?"

Bolan hated having no plan, particularly now that the woman's life was tossed into the equation. Another long look, and the warrior watched as they eased up another car length. Bristling with antennas and bearing a satellite dish, he knew that was no Mob van.

Professional trouble was on their bumper.

It was one thing, he knew, to cut down criminal thugs who often packed more mouth than punch. But the men behind them were black ops, stone-cold killers, with the training, expertise, experience and technology to ruin Bolan's night. More times than he cared to remember, he'd dealt with faceless black ops, men who took blank checks from various intelligence agencies, had no identities, were ghosts in the routine machinery of society. Whether DOD special, NSA, CIA, they seemed to believe they were not only above the law, but they were the law. They wrapped themselves up in what they considered to be the holy shroud of national security. No life was too innocent to spare if that meant protecting or furthering the agenda of their shadow masters.

In a way, they were much like himself, Bolan thought, but with one glaring difference. They didn't care about collateral damage, even if that meant wantonly spilling blood on American soil.

As far as the Executioner was concerned, they weren't much of a cut above Marelli.

And he would treat them likewise.

A plan, desperate and dangerous for all concerned, came to mind, and Bolan began laying it out.

"WHO ARE THESE GUYS? That's the broad, but where's Tony? I thought Tony was bringing the broad?"

Mike Lambrisi watched as two big guys in black escorted Marelli's girlfriend through the front door, thinking their wheelman, Timoli, had posed questions for which there was one obvious answer.

Bartino and the others had been bagged by the law. Or had they? The two men in black didn't strike him as officialdom. Something in the way they moved, predatory maybe, or perhaps too cool, like they had grenades in their bellies, violence inside that could suddenly erupt. They acted sure of themselves, but not in the arrogant way of a wise guy, or a cop, either thumbing their noses at the law, or using a shield to back up their every play.

Lambrisi palmed his cell phone and punched in Bartino's number. His agitation—more with his partners than the mystery—mounting. From the back seat, Lou Gamboni, all three hundred plus pounds of him, wheezed, "What do we do, Mikey? You think the cops grabbed Tony? You think the cops know about the disk? What the hell could be so important about this disk anyway we need to be sitting on the broad's place round the clock? Man, I ain't eaten in hours. I gotta take a leak."

"Quiet," Lambrisi grated. "Both of you." Timoli nearly blotted out the windshield with a rolling wave of cigar smoke. "You're givin' me a friggin' headache here."

He hated this stakeout duty, too, but he was more sick and tired of their bellyaching than the interminable hours.

Lambrisi cursed and dumped the cell phone on the seat.

"No answer from Tony?" Gamboni huffed.

"Sound to you like I got through?"

"Damn, Mikey, what's with all the hostility?"

"Okay, I got an idea," Timoli said, sounding to Lambrisi as if he thought he'd just invented the lightbulb. "We already gave the guy at the desk his money to let us in."

"And?" Lambrisi posed, wondering what blinding light Timoli would hit them with.

"We go in, make our bones, so to speak."

"Cowboy the action, other words," Lambrisi growled. "Without Tony's say so?"

"Why not? He wants the disk, hell, everybody wants this disk, kinda makes me wonder what Marelli put on it."

Lambrisi scowled, but saw where Timoli was headed. "You thinking glory or a cash contribution from New York for its safe delivery?"

"Maybe both."

"Maybe neither, if you hold out on New York, assuming we get our hands on it."

Timoli picked up his Ingram MAC-10, the glint in his eyes shining behind the cloud. "Only one way to find out, Mike. Are we men or are we mice?"

Lambrisi grunted. The crews these days were packed with glory hounds, out for themselves, building reps, chasing their pleasure more than taking care of business. But Timoli made a good point, he conceded. If they sat there, did nothing, and New York found out they maybe didn't have the stones to do the dirty work when necessary, there wouldn't be enough left of them for the rats to chew on.

Lambrisi was on the verge of cutting them all loose when he saw two more figures in black walk up to the front doors.

"Who the hell are these guys?"

Lambrisi wished Timoli would stop asking questions that had no ready answers. They were doing something to the door. Lambrisi thought they could be picking the lock, but the one doing the work didn't move a muscle.

They were in. Lambrisi watched in disbelief as one

of the men in black pulled out a pistol with sound suppressor. It didn't take much imagination for Lambrisi to count their deskboy out.

"You see that?" Gamboni puffed. "He shot our boy!"

This was more than Lambrisi could comprehend. Two sets of men in black, one marching in right on the heels of the other, the second pair just blasting away.

Lambrisi gathered up his own Ingram and stuffed two spare 30-round clips in his waistband.

"At least we'll be hitting both of them from behind," Timoli said, as if that would make the bloody chore of waxing four guys any easier.

Now that it was decided, Lambrisi heard Gamboni rack home a 12-gauge round in his Ithaca shotgun.

"Anybody concerned about waking up the building?" Lambrisi said. "I'm talking cops?"

"We're here, Tony ain't, I say we roll, take our chances," Timoli said.

"Lou? You game to go the distance?"

"Count on it," Gamboni wheezed.

Lambrisi was out the door gathering steam as he hustled across the parking lot. With Gamboni huffing on his heel, Timoli jogging hard and grabbing the lead, Lambrisi searched the sprawling lot.

Clear.

But he didn't like it. All these mystery faces, Tony dropping off the planet. Plus he had the feeling they were being watched.

"Take a look at this."

Lambrisi skidded up behind Timoli, thought he was

talking about the young kid, wasted where he sat behind the lobby desk, but found his wheelman staring at the key lock.

"Damn near melted the whole thing off like hot butter."

It was true. Lambrisi saw the lock had been reduced to liquid.

Timoli reached out to open the door, hesitating, as if he were about to touch a snake. No scream from Timoli. Lambrisi wondered what kind of opposition they were faced with. Something warned him this would not bode well for the three of them, but the door was open.

Lambrisi entered the lobby and ordered, "We'll take the stairs. Think you can manage two flights, Lou?"

"Hell, yeah," Gamboni huffed.

"Ezekiel to Striker, come in."

Mini-Uzi in hand, Bolan followed the woman through the apartment door, took in the foyer at a glance and motioned for Gabriel to grab a fire position in an alcove off the side of the landing.

"Here," Bolan called to Gabriel, and tossed him a frag grenade.

"Get it," he ordered the woman, who hesitated. "Let's go. Now."

A gentle shove and she was on her way, leading Bolan to what he assumed was her bedroom. As he plucked the TAC radio off his belt, Bolan watched her delve under the mattress.

"Go, Ezekiel."

"A party of three, looks like Bartino's people, just walked in behind our two pros."

Five on the way, Bolan thought, which left two others on the premises, maybe more waiting outside the building. The woman produced the disk and handed it to Bolan, scowling.

"I copy, Ezekiel. Stick to the plan."

"Copy, Striker."

"Must be pretty damn important, since I assume Bartino and his goons were going to rough me up before they took it," Tina said sullenly.

"Trust me, they would have done a lot worse than just slap you around."

Tina grumbled, "And, no, I couldn't get on. I don't know the access code."

Bolan took her by the arm and led her into the living room. It was less than two minutes since the blacksuit called Ezekiel informed him the pros had breached the building. The warrior could feel them coming. There was no other way, in his experience, to retrieve the disk than march right in, the hellhounds on their heels. If they wanted to bulldoze the action, then Bolan would be waiting.

They did.

Bolan was slinging the stripper behind a couch when the muffled crunch of a small C-4 charge blew in the front door.

MARELLI BURNED WITH ANGER and resentment, feared he was going to take the mother of all screwings. He didn't mind the big guy giving him a belt to the chops, nor wasting Bartino and the others, all of whom he knew—or so he'd heard the rumor—badmouthed him, thinking his rep was overinflated.

Punks, all of them. Try walking a day in his big shoes.

No, the way his nightmare began, Feds looking to snuff him on Cabriano's orders and cash, then a so-called agent of the U.S. Department of Justice running around racking up the body count, he figured it was time to fly. Whether or not the big shooter kept his promise about seeing Marelli still got full immunity no longer mattered.

The disk had been his only leverage. Once they got their mitts on it they could dictate the terms, tighten the clamp until he squealed for mercy.

He could just hear the words now. "Sorry about that, Jimmy. Deal's off the table. You're going away for life. No book deal, no movie, no beach, no broads."

Up yours.

Marelli knew the action was heating up again. The black-clad shooter with the HK subgun taking his orders from the big guy was already out the side door.

Leaving him all alone with the driver.

Marelli was torn between going for the wheelman or diving out the door. Say he clocked the wheelman, a double-fisted clobbering to the side of the head, snatched his side arm, then maybe put one through his brain. Take the wheel, drive out of Miami. He still had a couple of wise guys in south Florida he could trust.

He was in launch mode, legs tensing, the wheelman rolling them down the north side of the condo, when the gun flew out of nowhere.

And in his face.

"Going somewhere?"

THE FARM'S BLACKSUITS were professional military men, handpicked by Buck Greene, Brognola and Price, from the elite corps of Special Forces, Delta, SEALs, Marine Recon, Rangers and, occasionally, certain law-enforcement agencies. Not only were they the best of the best, they were sworn to secrecy when signed on by the Farm.

No loose tongue had ever flapped about the ultra-covert agency, all blacksuits professional to a fault.

And the one called Gabriel lived up to billing.

One adversary came in blasting, a spray-and-pray barrage that might have made a lesser man flinch. Tina understood round two of screaming her lungs off, but she was muted when the blacksuit's steel egg blew the competition away.

That left maybe one, Bolan thought, if he'd kept himself shielded from the brute force of the blast. Only one way to determine that, as the soldier yanked Tina to her feet, hauled her to the blacksuit.

"Take her," Bolan ordered Gabriel. "Stay behind."

Opting for two-fisted measuring of the enemy, the Executioner unleathered the Desert Eagle. As dust and plaster rained down, Bolan heard the groan, then saw the shredded enemy reeling into the door. He was quick, likewise opting for the double whammy of HK-Beretta, but Bolan beat him to the punch. A few rounds snapped past the Executioner's ears, but the black op couldn't quite bring the warrior on target. Skin flayed by shrapnel, he was nothing but pain and senselessness, and Bolan put him out of his misery. The Desert Eagle reared, tunneled a bloody fist high in the chest. Whirling, the black op held on, firing both weapons wild. Bolan hit him with a rising burst up the back.

Problems three, four, five, he was sure, were in the vicinity.

LAMBRISI KNEW they'd made a mistake as soon as the blast blew out the door and spun the two-fisted shooter away from the wall. Whoever these guys were, they were packing serious heat. Figure professional soldiers. He knew the three of them were outclassed.

But try telling that to Timoli.

The sight and smell of blood seemed to charge Timoli, the wheelman taking the lead, worked up into a frenzy when the mangled shooter went sailing across the hall. Lambrisi figured him down and out.

Lambrisi glimpsed a huge silver hand cannon jutting like some wand of doom out of the roiling smoke. It thundered, making Lambrisi realize the tattered heap on the far side of the hall hadn't given up the ghost.

He did when his head exploded, though. A great wash of blood and brains painted the white stucco wall like giant new wave splatter art.

"Hey…wait for me!" Gamboni said, lagging behind. Lambrisi wanted to laugh at the absurd notion the fat man even wanted a piece of this horror.

Whether the doomsday slayer inside the door sensed Timoli coming or felt the thundering drum of his shoes, Lambrisi would never know. And for all of his blustering Timoli never fired a shot.

The big guy whipped around the corner. A handgun that looked the size of a howitzer to Lambrisi unleashed two maybe three rolling peals of thunder. Lambrisi howled as the retort pierced his eardrums.

It was a flash of a face, carved in granite, blue eyes like two chips of ice, then a storm of bullets was blowing past Lambrisi. There was a split second when he realized he hadn't been hit, found it damn strange. The pro had made a mistake. Lambrisi was hell-bent on making him pay the ultimate price, finger hitting the trigger—

He heard the roar of Gamboni's shotgun from behind. He wanted to laugh, aware in an instant what the ice-eyed shooter had done. But it was impossible to laugh. He felt his body flying down the hall, when his lungs were blown out of his chest.

BOLAN COULD ONLY IMAGINE the treachery, the blood on the hands of the black ops. Whoever they pledged allegiance to didn't matter to the Executioner. Whether selling dual-use technology or radioactive waste for a dirty bomb, it all boiled down to one thing.

Treason.

On that grim note, he figured into every black op life a little pain and blood must fall.

He found Ezekiel and Nehemiah already working on the problem. Taking the lead, Bolan angled east, his blacksuits engaged at the deep end of the front lot with the enemy. Nehemiah had been the jump-man, bailing the van to come up the enemy rear once Ezekiel blocked their vehicle. Both sides were blazing away with subguns, the enemy duo trapped in their van. Ezekiel and Nehemiah were in the process of a leapfrog act, holding back on the triggers on their subguns, blistering the enemy wheels, stem to stern. One hardman tumbled out the driver's door and swept his Uzi in Bolan's direction. A line of parked cars provided the soldier with cover as the avalanche of lead blasted through windows, punching metal. A sharp grunt, then a howl, and Bolan saw two, maybe three spurts of dark fluid shoot from the hardman's upper chest. Mini-Uzi in one hand, the Desert Eagle in the other, Bolan cut loose with a double-clobbering that kicked the hardman into the van's side. As he folded and hit the deck, Bolan, with Gabriel bringing up the rear and Tina in tow, sidled to the far end of the van. He hit the other side of the bumper, just in time to find Nehemiah was number two, a line of 9 mm rounds ripping the hardman up the chest, driving him down the side of the van.

Bolan leaped over the fallen enemy, charging for their ride. Already he heard the wail of sirens in the distance.

He heard Nehemiah curse.

And Bolan discovered their next problem. Turning, ordering his people to get on board, he heard the huffing and puffing, three cars down. The mammoth hand cannon out and ready, Bolan whipped around a parked SUV and thrust the weapon in Marelli's face.

"Going somewhere?"

Marelli scowled. "Guess not."

BOLAN HANDED GABRIEL the disk as Tina boarded the Gulfstream jet.

It had taken a good hour for Price to hammer out the details on the detainment of Marelli and Tina, and another fifteen minutes for Bolan to explain the facts of life to both.

The Executioner was anxious to be on his way.

He was expected in Colombia, his own Gulfstream fueled and ready to fly.

Marelli hesitated at the ramp-ladder and gave Bolan a long look. "So this is it, huh?"

"And after all we've been through."

"I still got my deal, right?"

"If you ask me that one more time, I'll shoot you right here."

"Tina stayin' with me?"

"No conjugal visits on this go-round."

Marelli grunted. "You're a peach of a guy."

"Get going, Marelli."

"Anything else, Colonel?" Gabriel wanted to know.

Bolan turned, began heading for his Gulfstream,

threw a thumb over his shoulder. "Just make sure you take the trash with you."

It was the last Bolan ever hoped to see the likes of Jimmy Marelli.

Good damn riddance.

13

Jorge Quintero didn't see where they needed this deal. The truth was, he found it all distracting and dangerous nonsense. If not for his older brother, Fabio, who had, in essence, built the empire with his own sweat and blood, and who had more than once saved his life during an ambush by rivals, the younger Quintero would send them all packing. He had never quite understood his brother's unquenchable hatred of Americans. Fabio often railing that it wasn't enough to destroy their country with white poison. No, he wanted to see the Yankees attacked by the invisible force of terror, their streets running in blood, heaped with the dead and dying, weapons of mass destruction claiming lives by the thousands, the tens of thousands. Try to explain to Fabio that had already been happening in America for over three decades now. Their infrastructure, from families to entire communities, had been under the onslaught of cocaine and heroin for so long, they had, in effect, unraveled America from within. If he did not respect Fabio so much, if he did not owe him his very life…

Dressed in his safari outfit and broad-brimmed hat, he built another Scotch and water while working on his second cigar. Checking his diamond-studded Rolex watch, he decided he'd kept the gangster and the four American intelligence operators waiting long enough. The ten Saudis had been in the guest house, near the airfield, for more than a day now, making impatient noise about how they needed their own affairs concluded here. When would the other parties arrive? How did he know, Quintero thought. The American operators would call when they called, the shipment, as he understood it, was already packed up and en route. Relax, he told them. Take a swim.

Drink in hand, he was in no mood to play host, not with the number of bad questions about the disappearance of Hildago and his New York crew hanging over his head. Weighted down with the stainless-steel .50-caliber Magnum Desert Eagle on his hip, he nodded at Calabro to hold the door open for him. The world was becoming a more complex and strange place by the day, he decided. He longed for the simpler times, when the biggest concern was creating new routes and distribution points in America. When it was just the business of funneling merchandise and fattening their bank accounts.

These days, they were dealing with all manner of rabble, including American agents willing to sell radioactive waste to Mideast terrorists. And for what price? A stinking ten million was their cut off the top, and that included eight hundred kilos that were to go with the Saudis to be distributed on their end to other terror organizations.

Madness.

He found them gathered in what he called the Show Room. The sprawling teak-walled den was choked with animals he'd dropped by his own hand and had mounted for display. The gangster was paying particularly keen attention to the sixteen-foot crocodile he'd shot and killed on the Nile. There were exotic birds, a caiman and an anaconda, but the lion, the elephant and the Asian tiger were his personal favorites.

Quintero strolled into the middle of the room, claimed a white-leather couch for himself. His soldiers, many of whom were FARC guerrillas, were eyeing the strange group meandering about. He had allowed the intelligence operators to keep their subguns. Since his estate was patrolled and protected by close to a hundred men, he figured if they wanted to commit suicide then so be it. At first he found it rude that one operator elected to keep his helmet with black visor on, under his roof, hiding his face. Now he just wanted to be rid of all of them. But he had his own orders from Fabio.

"You kill all these yourself?"

The gangster sounded nervous to Quintero, seeming to go out of his way to admire his collection. "Yes," Quintero told him. "All of them."

Cabriano nodded. "Bet you made some taxidermist rich."

"Very."

"Enough small talk," the helmeted operator said. "My people just radioed, they're—"

"Yes, yes. We know. Ten minutes away. I have already cleared them to land," Quintero replied.

"So, let's go meet the Saudis," the agent said.

"Not so fast," Quintero said to Cabriano. "I understand our money has not left New York. Explain."

"I, uh, I had some unforeseen trouble the other night. We were hit by the Justice Department."

"And you are telling me, what? The American government has the Quintero brothers' money?"

Cabriano ran a hand over the elephant's hide. "I'm afraid so, but, before you get yourself all worked up, I should be able to reimburse you for the last shipment from some holdings the casino has in offshore accounts."

Quintero chuckled, sipped his drink, smoked. "Dummy companies, you mean, with bogus stockholders."

"Not all of them. Hey, Jorge, look, I lost my ass, too."

"We are talking a sizeable amount of cash if I understand correctly. In the neighborhood of fourteen million."

"We can work it out."

"I'm not here to talk about your drug business," the helmeted agent interrupted.

Quintero saw the man's gloved fist tighten around his subgun, and wondered if he and his comrades were crazy enough to start shooting up the room, surrounded as they were by twenty of his best fighters.

"You are here," Quintero said, growing tired of the agent's machismo stand, "as guests in my country. I suggest you pay some respect where respect is due. As for this arrangement with the Saudis, I am not in favor of it. If my brother, Señor Cabriano, had not done business with your father for so long, with so much profit and no grief, I would urge him to sever all ties with your organization. We Colombians prefer to use our own people in these matters anyway."

"Hey, look, Quintero, I got some problems back in New York but I'll handle them," Cabriano said.

"See that you do. As for the sudden and mysterious disappearance of Hildago and his men, I will discover the truth. Should it turn out you had something underhanded to do with it…"

Quintero left it hanging, but the fear in the gangster's eyes told him he wasn't up for going to war.

"I'm sure your boy will turn up," the agent said. "Now, can we take care of this business with the Saudis?"

Quintero rose. "By all means."

GROGEN KNEW HIM only as the Man with the Power. He was a god among the mere mortals of black ops intelligence, a killing ghost, no name, no identity, no past.

Nothing but a bad rep preceding him.

The helmet with visor shield never left the man's head, and when he spoke, handed out orders, anyone with any good sense listened. It was still the man's show. Grogen watched as the Saudis trudged from one of three huge red-tiled, white-stuccoed guest houses. Ten in all, four lugged nylon body bags, stuffed, he hoped, with their ten million. There was a lone space suit among the contingent, with a small instrument in hand that Grogen assumed was a Geiger counter.

Grogen wanted out of Colombia, back to the sanity of the States. He wanted to get as far away as possible from the eight drums. When they uncapped that poison, he knew the odor alone could knock a man off his feet.

The cargo was already rolled out of the gunship. Grogen caught the Colombian narcotrafficker throwing him funny looks as he kept backing away from the drums, his men removing the lead shields, getting ready for the Saudis to inspect.

While he waited on the Saudis to make their area, Grogen took in the landscape. They were north of Cali, in Quintero country, run by FARC rebels who, in turn, were owned by the cartel. Where llanos ended, rain forest took over, ringing what Grogen had heard was a three-hundred-acre estate. The drug lord's second home here was used chiefly for business. Three mountain ranges rolled up from Ecuador like giant anacondas. It was green, all around, rolling hills swaddled in broccoli-shaped trees.

That, he thought, was a problem.

And Grogen had an itch between his shoulder blades, warning him they were being watched. Forget the army of FARC guerrillas, spread all over the estate. There were antiaircraft batteries and machine-gun nests hidden in the edge of the jungle and jutting from the hangars around their airfield. It was no secret the CIA, DEA and U.S. Special Forces were entrenched down here. Tack on all the guerrilla armies, the graft and corruption, the fact that kidnapping was a major industry all by itself, all the bombings, murders of judges and cops who wouldn't be bought...

Grogen felt the weight of his weapon over his shoulder as the Saudis moved for the drums. And the Man with the Power wanted to know if they'd brought their money.

BOLAN HAD BEEN ATTACHED to a DEA-Special Force outfit code-named Dragon Company. Ostensibly they were military advisers, down here spraying the coca fields, raiding labs, working with Colombian authorities, training and so forth, but Bolan knew different.

Everyone knew where the drug lords were, where the labs were located in the jungles. The Colombian authorities knew all the shipping routes, much of the narcotics still flowing through neighboring Panama to the northwest. They knew the cartel used legitimate business as fronts to launder its dirty billions, much of Colombian officialdom still taking a fat envelope now and again. The DEA was sometimes thrown a nice bone to gnaw on, a big catch of a narcoshark maybe, a ton or two of coke seized, or a major lab burned down.

Everyone knew, but no one wanted to stop it. Why? Money.

And it was said, Bolan thought, that cocaine was still Colombia's number-one export, surpassing coffee.

All that was minutes away from changing, Bolan knew, as he pressed silently on into the jungle.

Major Horn had his orders, and Bolan could only imagine the man's thoughts that he had to turn over his force to Colonel Brandon Stone, and any problems with that, there was a number at the White House to call. Not only that, but Bolan was there to turn the covert war on drugs into overt slaughter.

Clad in dark green jungle fatigues, M-16/M-203 combo in hand, the warrior was weighted down in full combat regalia.

He moved in on the opposition from the east, eyes alert for patrols, booby traps. The numbers waiting were staggering. Between Quintero's army of FARC rebels and hired thugs, the Saudis, then the black ops force...

Well, that was why Bolan had a flying armada of gunships on standby. The transponder painted him on the screen of the major's Black Hawk, Bolan counting off the doomsday numbers, down to three minutes now.

He needed to hustle, get in position. A simple pager signal would let the major know to swoop down, blasting.

It had taken hours for Bolan and Horn to hammer out the attack plan, perusing sat and aerial pictures. But they both agreed on the threat to American national security from Colombia, and the good major pledged Bolan his full cooperation.

They agreed that for once, maybe the good guys could make a difference, or at least punch a hole in the enemy's armor.

Bolan would have preferred a night strike, but with all the enemy parties gathered on the airfield in broad daylight...

Take them as they came, they were all fair game.

CABRIANO KNEW he was going to get screwed in the deal.

He checked himself again in the black-tinted glass of the GMC, feeling as if he were vanishing before his very eyes. The fear and anxiety were bad enough, but heap raw anger on top of it all, and he was jumping out of his skin. Or he was shrinking inside himself, stewing over what bad thing would happen next.

He watched as the Man of Power ordered three of his men to begin hauling the Saudis' money toward the big cargo plane parked outside the hangar. It looked like they were negotiating, one of the Saudis flapping his arms, his mouth working overtime, in a snit. There were new black ops along for the trip, eight by his last count, all of them toting subguns, looking right through him when they bothered to look his way at all.

What the hell? Was he the invisible man?

No. He was a dead man, once Quintero found out Hildago and his New York boys had been with him when they were cut to ribbons in the Catskills. Or maybe there was a way out. After all, the helmeted agent was the one who killed them. Say he caught a moment alone with Quintero, explained the situation. The drug lord wanted out of this situation, dealing radioactive waste to terrorists. Understandable, it was time to get back to real business.

Maybe there was still time to conjure up plausible rationales. The space suit was just stepping up to the first drum, Geiger counter in one hand, wrench in the other working to twist off the cap.

"I'd be real careful how you handle that stuff."

It was one of the new ops, Cabriano heard. He wondered why the guy kept easing back, getting more distance from the drums. Cabriano was fifty or sixty yards from the inspection, but decided a few more feet couldn't hurt. When he caught a whiff of the toxin, heard gagging all around, he backpedaled another twenty feet in a hurry. Whatever that poison, it was like nothing he'd ever smelled. He couldn't even begin to describe it.

"What's your problem?" The new op was glaring at him.

"Right now, it's fresh air," Cabriano growled back. "So hold your nose."

BOLAN FOUND THEM gathered near the drums.

Picture perfect for what he had in mind.

He punched in the numbers to get Major Horn into the play, then took up the M-16. Figure a hundred yards to the south, nestled in brush at the edge of the tree line, enemy numbers were packed tight. A few 40 mms to start the big bang would carve the numbers by twenty to thirty guns.

Problem was, **this w**ould prove no easy chore. The compound was immense, with buildings staggered around three hundred acres. Between runners, the FARC army...

The plan was to blow the place off the earth.

No prisoners.

No time like the present, Bolan decided, curling his finger around the M-203's trigger.

They wanted a dirty bomb, they would get it.

14

With two Gulf wars and enough blood of terrorist scum on his hands to fill a lake, Grogen knew all about the calm before the storm.

In fact, two incidents tipped him off it was poised to go to hell.

First, the birds went into a sudden uproar, a hundred yards south, a rainbow of feathers, a squall of caws hitting the air in that direction. Second, three FARC guerrillas tore in from the north in a Hummer. They hopped out, ran up to Quintero, pointing their arms north. He didn't know much Spanish, but Grogen could read body language and understood enough to know a fleet of helicopters was on the way.

Quintero began cursing, fuming at the Man with the Power.

"I'm telling you, Quintero," Grogen heard the helmeted man growl, deciding a few more steps back were in order. "They're not mine. You have DEA problems, it's because you and your brother—who, I notice, is mysteriously AWOL—are drug dealers."

Grogen slipped the subgun off his shoulder. The

drug lord was railing now at his men about conspiracies, that American intelligence operators had set him up. The Saudis didn't look too thrilled to Grogen, either. The terror leader he knew as Rafiq Khalad opened a large nylon bag, hauling out an AK-47. The other Saudis were digging out assault rifles, but Grogen was watching the jungle to the south when—

It flew out of nowhere, and Grogen was already turning and running. He was pumping his legs when the missile impacted dead center in his worst fear.

BOLAN THOUGHT IT IRONIC that in a way he was right back where the campaign began. Sure, different country altogether, but he was once again blowing a hellstorm through the same cut of jackals. Some of the faces had changed, but the Farm had provided him with a file on the gathered parties. The Saudis were well-known terror financiers, have beaten American intelligence at every turn—until now.

It didn't escape Bolan's eye that Fabio was not on hand, but the Executioner already had a line on the older brother's locale.

Bolan cranked up the blast furnace of a 40 mm tempest.

Downrange, they were shrieking like the damned and Bolan quickly found out why. Some of the radioactive material showered about fifteen unfortunate cannibals out of the gate. If he didn't know better, Bolan would have said the flesh was melting off their bodies.

A few drums were left standing, and Bolan knew Major Horn had his own HAZMAT team ready to scoop up the waste.

CABRIANO FROZE at the sight of men wailing and thrashing on the ground. Those who took a bath in the stuff at ground zero appeared to be melting, or, rather, he judged, the flesh was oozing off their bodies. All of them were now without clothing. The odor of the poison was so strong that Cabriano retched.

He staggered toward the motor pool. A stampede, in fact, was already underway. FARC, the black ops, Saudis, everyone wanted to get the hell away from the raining toxin. He turned, searching the horror show, and saw the helmet melting off the spaceman's head. At first, he wasn't sure what he saw, straining his eyes. No, that was a grinning skull being revealed when the goo of his helmet rolled off. A screaming death's-head went silent, his former tormentor collapsing.

He saw men hopping into vehicles, then heard a storm of cursing. What the hell was this? They couldn't crank the engines. He wanted to try one for himself, so he threw open the door to a GMC, found keys in the ignition. He twisted. Nothing. Not a cough, not a sputter.

Cabriano felt hands clawing into his shoulder, felt himself go airborne out the door. He hit the ground, looked up and found a black op aiming his subgun in his face.

"I oughta kill you, Cabriano."

"What is that shit?" Cabriano screamed, more terrified of taking a bath in the toxic garbage than having his brains blown out.

"You wouldn't believe me if I told you!"

Cabriano let the black op drag him off the ground and thrust him toward the big cargo plane. They were getting out of there, that was all that mattered. Whatever waited him next...

He didn't even care about the money anymore. Just get him out of Colombia, back to Brooklyn.

"DRAGON LEADER to Ground Force One, come in!"

Bolan palmed his TAC radio, forced to shout through the static of Horn's voice. "Ground Force One here. You're breaking up."

"We're having instrument failure. I barely have your position painted."

"Hostiles have gone rabbit. Blanket the airfield and motor pool with everything you have, then start putting troops on the ground. Keep some distance from the shooting gallery. Whatever the substance in question is, it's shutting down engines. Copy that."

"Roger."

Bolan moved out of the jungle and dropped another bomb down the M-203's gullet. From the north, he saw the flying armada bearing down. Between the six Apaches and ten Black Hawks they owned the skies. The antiaircraft batteries, Bolan saw, were the first logical targets. Fiery mushroom clouds knocked out rooftop perches on hangars, then the pylons on the Apaches began flaming out more Hellfires, locking onto the motor pool and the cluster of planes.

Bolan didn't bother counting the dead already strewed near the initial strike zone.

There was more to come, he knew, and aimed for the last few drums.

"WHAT DO YOU MEAN the engine won't start?"

Cabriano listened as the black op screamed up the hull. The pilot, he assumed, was standing outside the hatch, a dumbfounded look on his face. One nightmare after another, it was more than Cabriano could bear. If he could find Quintero, if the drug lord was even alive...

Cabriano wheeled and ran down the ramp. He heard the black op screaming and cursing after him, waited for bullets to rip into his back.

A search of the horror stage, and Cabriano turned to stone at yet another unexplainable nightmare.

A green vapor appeared to fan out from the blast site. Mummylike figures were weaving ahead, but the mist seemed to chase them down. They cried out, clutching their throats, then grabbing at their eyes, falling to their knees. And the vapor, he saw, was rolling his way, spiking his nose with a stench he could imagine belonged in the deepest bowels of Hell.

He turned in every direction. Men were scattering pell-mell. Looking toward the drug lord's mansion in the distance, he made out the safari getup.

"Wait! Quintero!"

Cabriano bolted, heard the rattle of subgun fire from

behind, then the earth began erupting in explosions. The shock waves nearly bowled him off his feet, but terror and the sight of more men melting before his eyes galvanized him into speed he didn't think he had.

"Wait! Quintero!"

GROGEN BOUNDED down the ramp. The Apaches, he saw, were hard at work, Hellfires and chain guns eating up aircraft, turning vehicles into steel coffins where runners still attempted to fire up engines. He knew they were painted. FARC rebels were spraying autofire at the flying armada, then were cut down by long roaring waves of doom. The gunships were holding their position, staying clear of the dispersed waste.

Running, he found four of their own contingent, armed and likewise bolting from the doomed plane. Where to go? And who to shoot? The noxious fumes of the mystery waste were knotting his stomach as he took in the sea of bodies. A green cloud, he observed, hung over the field of carnage. One by one, more victims toppled, bone glistening where flesh had been stripped off.

Pumping his legs, he spotted Cabriano closing in on Quintero in the distance. They were fleeing for the safety of the big house on the hill. Figure Quintero had an escape valve in the event of a raid. Go west then, he decided, this game was dead.

The earth roaring behind, Grogen looked back. Balls of fire marched up the hull of their cargo plane. He flinched at the brilliance of the firestorm as it reduced their ride to flying junk.

Now they were definitely stuck in Colombia, Grogen cursing the day he volunteered for this assignment.

He kept running, scouring the hell to the south. Another blast ripped through the last few drums. They were shooting for the sky, metallic comets that...

Grogen went limp at the sight of those rockets streaking his way. Through the smoke overhead he glimpsed the mangled lids flying off, steel Frisbees that whirled on, then the contents were spewing.

Grogen sprinted, his screams trailing him. He looked up, hoping he was clear, but found blue sky gone green and falling on top of him.

IT WOULD HAVE BEEN better, or at the least quicker, for the men on the run if they'd remained in the cargo plane, gone up in smoke and flames with the brief Hellfire barrage. The end result was a hell unlike any Bolan could ever recall witnessing.

As it stood, they took a toxic waste shower, hollering like banshees, writhing on the ground, burning up from invisible fire. A couple of them shouted out for deliverance from a God Bolan could be sure they'd never believed in.

It was something Bolan could never explain, as he veered around the exploding green cloud. The stench alone was beyond any battlefield miasma he'd ever encountered. Then the waste, and the vapor, literally ate the flesh off bone, as quick as a man getting dipped in a vat of acid.

Whatever it was, Bolan knew if it fell into terrorist hands and they unleashed a dirty bomb laced with the toxin the horror he found churning before him would have been shot up on a scale...

But that would not happen.

He was there, and the enemy was going down.

The Executioner rammed a fresh clip into the M-16. The screams alone would have chilled a man not accustomed to the horrors of war. But even Bolan had to admit what he heard and saw took death to a whole new level.

This was Hell on Earth.

They cried out in a mixed bag of Arabic, Spanish and English, the damned, blind and stripped of flesh, reeling from the mist.

Bolan spared a full clip of mercy bursts.

Dragon Company had demolished anything that could fly or drive away. The toxic cloud had done most of the dirty work for them. Sometimes divine justice prevailed in mysterious ways.

Horn had his orders, and Bolan went in search of fresh game.

The mansion on the hill was the next target, the Executioner heading that way, double time.

The line on Jorge Quintero was that he was something of a big-game hunter, bagging everything from white sharks to bull elephants. But the truth, Bolan knew, was the man always kept a huge entourage of snipers close by when the killing of an animal for his trophy collection needed to be done.

It figured.

Briefly he recalled part of a conversation with Major Horn while taking in the gathering of armed vultures near the pillared front entrance to the mansion. The

Quintero Cartel had been protected by the Colombian power base for years. The cartel donated huge sums to various charities, built schools, hospitals, all of them, of course, erected in their name. Bolan knew he'd never flush out all the vipers down here, likewise angrily aware the whole truth about this campaign would never see the light.

The Executioner advanced on the Quintero stronghold, watching as the Hellfires began peppering the mansion, the Black Hawk door gunners mowing down any ground resistance.

15

"I blame you for this disaster!"

"Me? How do you get that?"

Cabriano was stunned by the accusation. Given the rage, though, that exploded at him from Quintero, he felt it wise to attempt to weather the drug lord's storm.

Quintero had led him back into the Show Room, where the rebels were loading duffel bags with cash, notebooks, ledgers.

They were under siege. The entire house right then was shaking as the gunships that had razed what he figured was nearly a mile stretch of airfield and damn near a hundred men, pounded away from all directions. Quintero was pulling up stakes, that much was clear. Cabriano figured there had to be a tunnel out of the mansion. He hardly wanted to glue himself to the trafficker's coattails under these conditions, but Quintero was his only hope.

"Your trouble became my trouble! You could not take care of your own affairs, you brought agents, CIA, NSA, who knows into my life! I had a good life!" Quintero was screaming at him.

Cabriano wished for two things as he counted up the number of FARC goons in the room, five in all. Realizing that Quintero was worked up into a murderous snit, he wanted an assault rifle.

And he wanted a phone.

Funny, he decided, what a man did, what he thought of when the end was near. Trouble was, he was torn between whether he'd make his last call on Earth to his wife or mistress.

Maybe it didn't matter.

Cabriano listened to the endless chatter of autofire from some point beyond the open doors, men screaming out the ghost. Plaster rained in his face. The trophy animals were rocking with the pitch and yaw of a house about to come down on their heads.

"My world goes up," Quintero yelled. "You go down with me!"

"What about your brother?"

"What about him?"

"We could use his help here!"

"He is at the laboratory, working to prepare your next shipment." Quintero laughed.

"Get us out of Colombia," Cabriano said, hating the note of pleading in his voice. "We wait this out, regroup. The black ops are all dead. The Saudis, too."

"Back to business as usual?"

"Why not?"

"Because, you fool, my brother and I are finished in Colombia. This is a blatant show of force, something which we have paid everyone short of God to protect us from!"

"Finished?"

And then the end came.

Quintero was pulling the huge hand cannon, Cabriano ready to dive for cover when the room blew up before his eyes.

THE FRAG BLAST LED Bolan into the drug lord's trophy room. Two full squads of DEA-Special Forces commandos had his back covered, the mansion ready to cave in any second. Bolan needed this wrapped, aware Fabio Quintero would be on high alert.

The savages had been embroiled in a heated argument. Bolan found a few FARC-stragglers loading up whatever Quintero thought he needed to make a clean break. No point in prolonging their misery and fear, the Executioner rolled into the room, M-16 blazing. Three FARC thugs were hacking their way out of the smoke, assault rifles firing wild.

Bolan diced them with a long raking, left to right, bodies slamming off the stuffed bull elephant.

Quintero stepped up to the plate, roaring something in Spanish, the Desert Eagle thundering, drowning out his words.

Marching on, Bolan hosed the drug lord with a burst to the chest. Quintero hammered his rhino trophy, bounced back, blood streaking his face, the handgun roaring. Then Bolan hit him with another burst to the chest and dropped him.

All done here, with one more Quintero savage on the loose.

Catching withering autofire from beyond the trophy room, Bolan moved toward the dead animals, stuffing and shredded cloth fluttering through the air. He took in the carnage, suddenly felt as if he'd aged ten years in two days. All the lives lost, including some good ones since the campaign began, and he briefly wondered how much of a difference had he made.

Tomorrow, more like the Quinteros would rise up, he knew. But he would be there, doing what he could to see those who wished to live in peace—not rape, rob or murder or gain an empire through crime—made it through another day. Another Cabriano would claim the crown of crime…

The groan snapped Bolan's head to the side. The M-16 swung toward the human wreckage on the floor. Bolan saw a pair of legs eaten up by shrapnel. A few steps in that direction, and he found Cabriano still breathing and holding on to Quintero's Desert Eagle.

Cabriano had to have sensed his presence, since Bolan watched as the mobster aimed a look of pure anger and hate his way.

"You? Who…are you?"

Bolan answered the question with a burst to Cabriano's chest, then raised Major Horn.

"I'm on my way out, Major. Let's saddle up before brother Fabio takes a long boat ride down the river."

"I suppose it wouldn't do any good, Colonel, to scratch the hit on their jungle compound for now, seeing as there's a fat whopping mess here to contend with?"

"You can clean up later."

"Okay, Colonel. It's your party, but it may be my funeral when you leave. I have the Colombian military to deal with when you walk off into the sunset."

"Where's the Major Horn I heard when I landed? The man who wanted to take the gloves off and declare total war on the traffickers and FARC?"

"Yeah, well, that was until I saw all these bodies that looked like they'd been dipped in acid."

"What you see spread around out there is the last of it."

"I hope to God you're right."

So did Bolan, but he wasn't about to raise phantom red flags.

There was slaughter work still to be done.

FABIO QUINTERO KNEW that nearly two decades on top of the cocaine heap was unheard-of. All traffickers, no matter how smart, how tough, how rich, had a life expectancy of ten, twelve years tops. That he—and brother Jorge—had survived and not been imprisoned, or worse, extradited to America, was a testament, he supposed, to the fact he believed in the hands-on approach to business.

For once, he had broken that rule, and now he feared it would cost him his world.

"Keep trying, dammit!"

"Sir, there's nothing but static on their—"

He wheeled on his radioman, felt his grip tighten on the Galil assault rifle.

"Understood."

He marched out of the command hut, silently urging his FARC work force to hurry up loading the fifty-kilo bales onto the transport trucks. They needed the shipment dumped on their gunboats, moved both up and down river and stashed in various safehouses in Cali and throughout the surrounding region before nightfall. Twenty distributors were demanding more product, and the Russians were due in Cali later that night.

A hundred worries and self-doubt flooded his thoughts. Because of Jorge's reluctance to carry out his wishes where their Mideast contact, the American mobster and the intelligence operators were concerned, pure stubbornness and pride had swayed him to leave his younger brother alone with the arriving parties. Mistake number one. He should have been there, since he had negotiated the deal with the mobster himself, though the intelligence operators had sought him out. And there the question of cutting American intelligence operators into the action lingered. Again, he figured pride got the better of him, thinking himself safe and secure in Colombia. Let them all come to him, he owned half the military and police, and those he couldn't buy ended up dead, along with their entire families.

Feeling the impatience and worry gnaw deeper, he began barking at his workers to load the trucks with greater speed. He scoured their sweaty scowls as they trudged bales from the lab.

And yet perhaps another mistake, Quintero thought. The lab itself was shoved back into the forest. The jungle canopy was a thick spiderweb tangle, but only directly over the canvas roof. He had other facilities, underground, but the cost to maintain labyrinthine labs was astronomical. Besides, here they were close to the river, with easy and quick access to his brother's airfield, then quick shipping routes north, through Panama. With all his informants in the military and police, many of whom worked with the Americans, he would be alerted well in advance, normally twenty-four hours before a raid was launched. In that event, product and precursor chemicals could be moved, the raiding party hitting a facility, stripped clean, the Americans left swatting at mosquitoes.

It had never failed before, he thought, striding toward the lead transport, snarling at his people to board.

He was grabbing the door handle when he heard a sound he feared as much as death. It descended from all points, the whapping squall of rotor blades appearing to blow the roof off the jungle canopy. He heard shouting in panic from the lab and turned that way as the first missile scored a direct hit in the heart of the facility.

MAJOR HORN HAD NOT achieved stellar success against the Quintero Cartel. After going through the Farm's intel, a few answers to the problem came to light. One word leaped to Bolan's mind.

Informants.

Each raid on the Quinteros' operations had been planned twenty-four hours before the event happened. That left an open window for the store to get hauled somewhere far away. Yes, there would be DEA, CIA down here, holding hands with the opposition, and whether or not Major Horn was planning his own future by lopping off a piece of the cocaine action was moot. If that was the case, he would be found out soon enough. Then there were the Colombian authorities, notorious for wearing the right public face, but in private unchaining the snakes.

With round one behind them, Bolan hit the jungle lab with the only real solution to the problem.

Another lightning tempest of Hellfires, bullets and commandos got the avalanche rolling.

Bolan bounded off the Black Hawk, the M-60 door gunner yammering out the heavy metal thunder. Dragon Company had the skies swarmed with gunships on all points, two more Hellfires pretty much vaporizing the lab. A firestorm gushed out, as ether and acetone ignited. Flaming human comets came wailing from the inferno.

Bolan turned his sights on the trio of transport trucks lurching off down the trail.

That would be Quintero.

The elder Quintero had a nasty surprise waiting when he hit the river.

Bolan fired his M-16 at armed FARC thugs, shooting from the hip, dusting four on the fly before he hit the trail. An explosion rocked the jungle behind Bolan.

Turning he found commandos leaping from the flaming hull of a Black Hawk going down, crashing its fiery descent through the jungle canopy.

The Executioner left Horn and commandos to nail it down, and gave chase to the last savage.

"HURRY! HURRY!"

Fabio Quintero cursed his mules, spewing all the fear and hatred he felt about the destruction of his lab from a force that shouldn't exist. He charged up and down the wooden wharf, torn between watching the sky over the river and railing for the workers to just hurl the bales into the gunboats.

He heard engines sputtering to life and caught the raging storm of death and destruction beyond the line of dense jungle vegetation.

He froze suddenly, warning bells gonging in his head. Why were there no helicopters over the river? Where were all the enemy commandos? Why was he standing there, alone, with his boat and two tons of product?

The two Apaches sailed out of nowhere. They looked like giant prehistoric birds to Quintero as it hit him what was happening.

He raged at the injustice of it all, knew the kingdom was about to go up in flames.

It did, as he hit the deck and the first missile blew a gunboat out of the water.

BOLAN STEPPED OFF the trail, M-16 chattering at armed figures scraping themselves off the matchstick ruins of the wharf. The Apaches soaring on down the river, the Executioner blew doomed opposition back into flaming trash pelting the water. From the raining debris of gunboats, a white mist floated behind the wreckage.

Bolan navigated a march, hugging the edge of the jungle tree line. One man was left, crabbing, Galil in hand, at the far edge of the wharf. As he closed in, he recognized the elder Quintero. The drug lord grunted, hauled himself to his feet. All these years the trafficker had reigned, escaping justice, either rough or at the hands of the law. Bribes, murders, or fleeing the country until the heat cooled, Bolan figured Quintero had worn a tainted crown long enough.

The drug lord snarled an oath, wheeled toward Bolan. Beyond the feral look in the eyes, the soldier read an unquenchable anger and hate, the man not wanting to give up the ghost. If Bolan let him walk, he would buy his way out, and back into the game of dispensing death and misery. But Quintero made his move, aiming his Galil with shaking hands.

The Executioner hit the M-16's trigger and blew Quintero into a watery grave.

Epilogue

"What? No bouquet of roses?"

Bolan found Brognola sitting halfway up in bed. The big Fed looked understandably gaunt and tired, but there was a shine to his eyes that told Bolan the man was grateful he—both of them—was still alive.

Bolan took a chair beside the man's bed. Brognola had a room to himself, the Justice Department even hooking up cable to his television. The big Fed was watching a news channel.

The doctor told Bolan it was a miracle how quickly Brognola was on the mend, the bullet having missed both heart and spine by less than an inch. Stranger things, Bolan knew, had happened.

For a few moments they sat in the kind of peaceful silence that only longtime friends could share.

"It's good to see you," Brognola said quietly.

"It's good to be here. By the way, the roses are Barb's department," Bolan told Brognola, and reached into his coat pocket. "She's on the way," he added, and held out three Havanas for Brognola's viewing pleasure.

THE DESTROYER

DARK AGES

LONDON CALLING...

Knights rule—in England anyway, and ages ago they were really good in a crisis. Never mind that today's English knights are inbred earls, rock stars, American mayors and French Grand Prix winners. Under English law, they still totally *rock*. Which is why Sir James Wylings and his Knights Temporary are invading—in the name of Her Majesty.

Naturally, Remo is annoyed. He is from New Jersey. So when Parliament is finally forced to declare the Knight maneuvers illegal, he happily begins smashing kippers...knickers...whatever. Unfortunately, Sir James Wylings responds by unleashing his weapons of mass destruction—and only time will tell if the Destroyer will make history...or be history, by the time he's through.